THE
FERGUSON RIFLE

THE
FERGUSON RIFLE

LOUIS L'AMOUR

BANTAM BOOKS
TORONTO · NEW YORK · LONDON · SYDNEY

THE FERGUSON RIFLE
A Bantam Book

PRINTING HISTORY
Bantam rack-size edition / March 1973
Louis L'Amour Hardcover Collection / September 1982

Library of Congress Cataloging in Publication Data
L'Amour, Louis, 1908–
The Ferguson Rifle
I. Title
[PZ3.L1937Fe]   [PS3523.A446]   813'.5'2   72-13698

If you would be interested in receiving bookends for
The Louis L'Amour collection,
please write to this address for information:

The Louis L'Amour Collection
Bantam Books
P.O. Box 596
Hicksville, NY 11801

ISBN 0-553-06232-8

Published simultaneously in the United States and Canada

PRINTED IN THE UNITED STATES OF AMERICA

0   9   8   7   6   5   4   3   2

THE
FERGUSON RIFLE

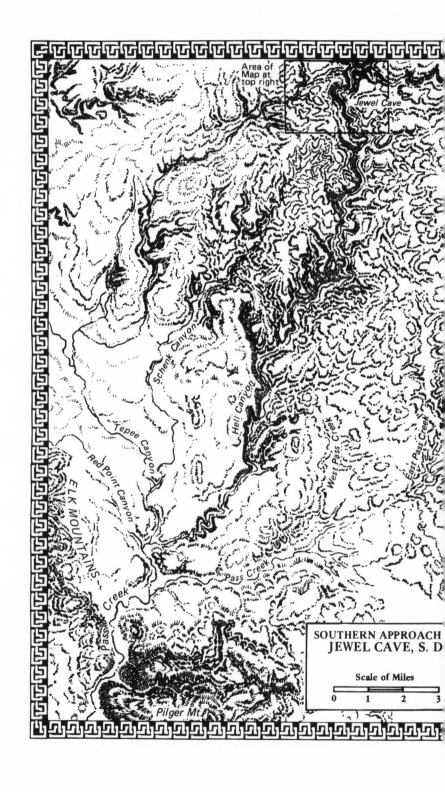

Area of
Map at
top right

Jewel Cave

Schenk Canyon

Hell Canyon

Tepee Canyon

Red Point Canyon

West Pass Creek

East Pass Creek

ELK MOUNTAINS

Pass Creek

Pass Creek

Pilger Mt.

**SOUTHERN APPROACH
JEWEL CAVE, S. D**

Scale of Miles

0   1   2   3

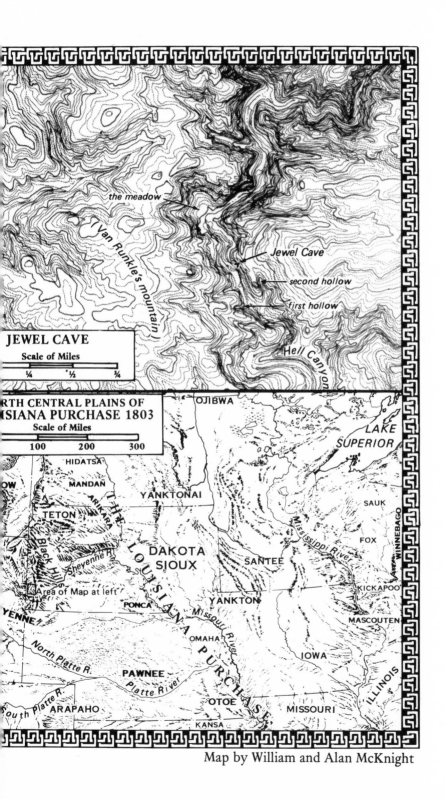

JEWEL CAVE

the meadow

(Van Runkle's mountain)

Jewel Cave

second hollow

first hollow

Hell Canyon

Scale of Miles

¼   ½   ¾

RTH CENTRAL PLAINS OF
ISIANA PURCHASE 1803

Scale of Miles

100   200   300

OJIBWA

LAKE SUPERIOR

HIDATSA

MANDAN

ARIKARA

TETON

YANKTONAI

SAUK

WINNEBAGO

Black Hills

Sheyenne R.

DAKOTA SIOUX

SANTEE

Mississippi River

FOX

Area of Map at left

KICKAPOO

YENNE

PONCA

YANKTON

Missouri River

MASCOUTEN

North Platte R.

OMAHA

IOWA

PAWNEE

Platte River

THE LOUISIANA PURCHASE

ou th Platte R.

ARAPAHO

OTOE

MISSOURI

ILLINOIS

KANSA

Map by William and Alan McKnight

ONE

My name is Ronan Chantry, and I am alone upon this land. I have long since crossed the Mississippi. No other rides with me, and the plains lie vast about. My eyes are toward the horizon where the sun sets in gold and crimson, an enormous sun like none my eyes have seen in the thirty years that have been mine.

What I loved is gone. What I lived for, vanished. I ride westward into an unknown land, toward what destiny I know not. It has ever been our way, we Chantrys, to turn westward when faced with grief and desolation.

I ride to lose myself, but can a man ever lose that which is in him? That which is blood and bone to him? That which has been his life?

Men have told me that I am a fool, that I ride only to my death, but if it is to be, then let it be.

My wife, my dearly beloved, is dead. My son, who was to grow tall and sire yet another generation of our family, is also gone, done to death by the flames from which he tried to rescue his mother.

Within me is emptiness; the studies to which I had given my life, abandoned.

1

I have a good horse, a small pack, an excellent knife, and I have the Ferguson rifle. That rifle, my constant companion since childhood, is all that remains of my past, that and a few precious books to stimulate my thoughts until . . . ?

The rifle was given to me when I was a small boy, presented by the man who simplified the loading mechanism and put into action the most efficient weapon of the century.

Major Patrick Ferguson demonstrated the weapon at Woolwich in June 1776. Four years later, he was killed at the Battle of King's Mountain, North Carolina.

The rifle was given me only a few weeks before his death, a truly marvelous weapon made and engraved by his own hand. It was one of the first to be loaded at the breech, and could be loaded and fired six times to the minute. In the almost twenty-five years since it came into my hands, I have seen no rifle to compare.

Ours was a poor cabin, and I stood by the gate holding the heavy musket with which I had barked a squirrel, watching a red-coated officer riding up the path from the road.

He looked at me sharply, then at my musket. "Lad, I am fair done in. Could I be having a drink from your well?"

He had a good face, a strong face. "Sir," I said, "you men of England have been my enemies, but I will refuse no man a drink. Will you come in, then?"

He glanced toward the house, wary of a trap. I had no idea of it then, but he was a much hated man, and a man known for his harsh opinions of the colonists.

"There's nought to fear," I said, and there was scorn in my tone. "My ma is ill within, and I must be about fixing her supper." I held up the squirrel, and not without pride.

He glanced at it, then at me. Riding through the open gate to the well, he dismounted to accept the water-filled gourd dipper from my hand. "Thanks, lad." He drank the cold water from the dipper, then refilled it to drink again. "There's no finer drink than this, lad. Hear it from a thirsty man."

He noticed the puzzled expression in my eyes as I looked at his horse. It was a fine animal, but it was his weapons that puzzled me. He wore a saber, and there were two horse pistols in scabbards, which was not unexpected, but he also carried two rifles, one of them carefully wrapped in an oiled cloth.

"What is it, lad?"

"Two rifles?" I said.

He chuckled, but his eyes were on my ancient musket. "If you can bark a squirrel with that," he said, "you must be an uncommonly good shot."

"I daren't miss," I admitted honestly. "When our powder and shot are gone, we must live on greens."

He finished his water, then led his horse to the trough. "May I pay my respects to your mother, lad? If you say no, I shall not intrude."

"She would enjoy it, sir. We have few visitors here, and my mother pines for them. Until she came here, she lived always among people."

My mother was a woman of rare beauty. It took me years and the viewing of many women before I really grasped how truly rare. She was pale now, and thin, lying in the old, high bed, but her hair was done on this day as upon every day of her life. She was ever groomed and neat, and much to my disgust, required that I be the same. The habit was well formed, and is with me still.

The major stepped into our cabin, removed his hat, and bowed. "I am Major Ferguson, ma'am, of His Majesty's Second Battalion, Light Infantry Highlanders. Your son was kind enough to provide me with a drink, and I wished to pay my respects."

"Will you be seated, major? I'm afraid we have little to offer, but if you would join me in a cup of tea?"

"I would be honored, ma'am. Honored, indeed. It is little we see of the ladies these days. Times are hard for a soldier, ma'am."

"And I would they were harder, major." Even as she said it, she smiled, taking the sting from the words. "You come unbidden to our country as you came unbidden to my other country."

"Your *other* country, ma'am?"

"I was born in Ireland, major, and grew up there. I came over the sea to marry my husband, whose family was known to ours."

"I am a Scotsman. Many of us, ma'am, did not approve of

the manner in which affairs were handled in Ireland. We do not make policy. That is the king's business."

"And a poor business he makes of it. But here, now! This is not fit conversation for a guest in my house. Ronan, would you pour tea for us, please?"

My mother's hair was red gold, and the silken bed jacket she wore had come from France, in a better day than this.

"If you will permit, ma'am"—the major accepted his tea—"I had not expected to find a gentlewoman in such a place. Not a woman of such obvious—"

"Breeding, major? There is no latitude or longitude for breeding. We who migrated from Ireland left much behind, often including the O or the Mac that preceded our names, but we did not leave our pride, nor, I hope, our good manners."

She smoothed the rough blanket with her hands as though it were satin or whatever she'd known in her younger years. "You travel far, major?"

"To join my command. It is twenty miles, I believe." As if reminded, he got to his feet. "I should prefer to remain, but the ride is long." He hesitated, and then said, "We shall not trouble your land much longer, ma'am. You have resisted us strongly, and at home there's a distaste for it."

"As well there might be," she said quickly, but smiling. "If you pass this way again, will you stop?" She smiled impudently. "The good Lord commands us to forgive our enemies, major, and I forgive you."

"Of course." He glanced at me. "The boy's father? Will he soon be home?"

"He was killed in the war, major."

"If there is anything I can do?"

"No, major. My son does very well. He is a skillful hunter and we shall do splendidly." She extended a slender hand. "Do stop by, major. You will be most welcome."

He took her hand, bowing gracefully, brushing her fingertips with his lips. "It was my pleasure," he said, stepping back, then another step, and turning he went out the door, putting on his hat as he did so.

There was a moment when he kissed her hand that I could

only stare, for I believed such things happened only in palaces or among great ladies and kings.

"See him to the gate, Ronan. He is a fine gentleman, and conducts himself as one."

Major Ferguson had gathered his reins and was stepping into the saddle when I came to open the gate. "Your mother is a great lady, lad, a great lady. She should not be living here, in this manner."

From his saddle he took the wrapped rifle, unwrapping it slowly. It was utterly new, unused, silver mounted, and engraved. I gasped.

"Handsome, is it not? I made it myself, for myself." He showed me how it was loaded for I had not seen a breech-loader before, nor the mechanism he had invented, for he told me that as he showed me the rifle. "Lad, I have a notion I shall not have long to use it, and there's no telling into whose hands it might fall. A fine lad such as you, who appreciates a good weapon and must provide for his mother . . . well, lad, you need a rifle, not a musket."

I could scarcely whisper. "It . . . it's for *me*?"

"It is." He put it into my hands.

"Sir"—I held it reverently as a father holds his firstborn child—"I cannot accept it. My mother would not permit it."

"Take it, lad. I shall be gone and there will be no way to return it." From his saddlebags he took a bag of shot and another of powder. "Do you take these too. You surely need them more than I, and before many hours are past, I shall be where there is little else.

"Care for it, son, and it will care for you. I ask only one thing. Keep it always, and never use it against the king."

When he had disappeared around the bend, I walked back to the cabin. When I showed it to mother, she reproved me gently. "You should never accept a gift unless you can return one of equal value, but when a gift is given, it should be accepted with grace."

She leaned back on her pillow, happier than I had seen her in many weeks. We had few visitors, most of them country people. Good, honest folk they were, but with few social graces, and none of them from the cities beyond the sea.

A few weeks later, we heard of the Battle of King's Mountain, and of the death of Major Ferguson.

We heard much of him later, for he had admirers on both sides of the line. He came of a distinguished Scottish family, was only thirty-six when killed, and had been in the service for twenty-one years.

The Ferguson rifle, which might have won the war in a matter of months, had been taken from his command and put into storage by General Howe after Ferguson had been wounded at Brandywine.

The rifle he left with us helped us through those bad times. Its accuracy was scarcely to be believed, and I became skilled in its use, acquiring speed in reloading. Each time I used it, I blessed the major.

When spring came at last, mother received a small legacy from a distant relative in Ireland and we moved to the vicinity of Boston and I took the Ferguson rifle along.

The woods lay not far from our home, and often I hunted there. The education I received and enriched by my own reading was an excellent one, and for a year I read law, but a meeting with Timothy Dwight convinced me I should become an educator and a writer of history. Yet now I rode westward into a wild land where the only education needed was that the land could provide.

The sun was gone, although light remained. With darkness near, I still had no camp, and the bald plains promised nothing.

Suddenly, as if born of a wish, there appeared a fold in the low hills. A grassy slope dropped away to a cluster of trees, dark now with evening, and I thought I detected the sheen of water.

Many were the warnings I had received. Water holes were few, used by all, and at any such place death might await. I had not hunted through my boyhood years for nothing, nor had scholarship robbed me of my senses. My nostrils caught the scent of woodsmoke, and I drew rein to listen.

At first I heard nothing, then the faint sound of horses cropping grass, and a crackle as from a fire. Standing in my stirrups, I peered through the leaves, but could see only the shine of light reflected from the seat of a saddle.

It was unlikely a saddle would be used by an Indian, but there were many dangerous men on the prairie, not all of them Indians by any means.

Rifle in hand, I walked my horse forward, calling out, as was the custom. "Halloo, the camp!"

"Come in with your hands empty!" The voice was matter-of-fact. "Or take a bullet through the brisket."

I drew up. "When I come in, gentlemen, it will be with my rifle in my hands, and if you want to start shooting, just open the ball!"

Somebody chuckled, and then said, "All right, all right! Come on in!"

Several men sat about a fire, and two of them had rifles in their hands. All wore buckskins; all had the appearance of frontiersmen. My dress alone would add a discordant note, for I wore a brass-buttoned blue coat, gray pantaloons with straps under the arches of my Hessian boots, and a starched white cravat. My hat was of the English round variety such as was worn by the young gentleman of fashion. Yet their eyes were on my rifle.

The Ferguson I carried was but thirty inches long; their own rifles looked to be forty-four inches at least.

" 'Light, stranger. Looks like you've come a fur piece."

"That I have." Rifle in hand I dismounted, keeping my horse between them and me.

One of the men chuckled. "Now that goes right with me. I like a careful man."

Tying my horse, I walked around him. "Possibly I am less careful than you suspect. My friends told me I was foolish to come out here alone."

"You're *alone*?" Startled, they stared at me. "Now that's hard to believe. You're four days' ride from a settlement, mister."

"Three . . . on this horse. You're the first living things I've seen, other than birds and insects."

My palm slapped the rifle. "Anyway, as long as I have this, I'm not quite alone."

The first man to speak indicated the rifle. "Don't know's I ever seen the like. Mind if I look?"

It was my turn to chuckle. "Gentlemen, if I allowed a chance acquaintance to take my gun from my hand, I'd be a lot greener than I am . . . and I am green."

Moving up to the fire, I held it for them to see. "This is a Ferguson rifle, given me by the inventor when I was a lad. It is a remarkably accurate, fast-shooting rifle."

A slim, dark young man seated near the Indian nodded. "I heard tell of them. Heard it said they can shoot six times to the minute."

"*Eight,* gentlemen, eight times if one is practiced." I glanced around at the group. "I'm Ronan Chantry, and I'm riding west to the Rockies. If you're going my way, I'd like to join you."

The lean dark man got to his feet. "I'm Davy Shanagan. Are you from the old country, then?"

"My mother was, and my great-grandfather, too."

"Sit, then, Ronan Chantry, and we'll talk of the western lands and what we'll do there. A man with a rifle that can be shot eight to the minute is welcome at any fire in the west."

The others agreed, but my eyes went to the Indian, whose eyes were on the rifle in my hands.

With a rifle like that, an Indian would be a big man among his own people.

It was something to remember.

TWO

D avy Shanagan glanced critically at my costume when I
joined him at the morning fire. "You surely ain't dressed
for the country." He glanced up at me as I warmed my hands.
"Chantry, d'you have any idea what you're up against? We're
westward bound, after fur. No tellin' what we'll find yonder."

"I trapped some, as a lad."

"You heard tell of this Lewis and Clark outfit? We figured if
they could go west, we could, too. We won't be crossin' trails
with them. They'll be much farther north, but James Mackay
crossed this country we're ridin' into, and he trapped fur
there."

"It won't be easy," I admitted. "There was a Spanish army
outfit marched north from Santa Fe to the Missouri, but Indians wiped them out when they got there.

"The Mallett brothers and six others went back the other
way. It's said they named the Platte. It's rough country, but
I've a notion we can make it."

Shanagan poked sticks into the flames. "Just about anywhere
a man goes, he'll find somebody has been there before him."
He glanced up at me again. "You up to that kind of travel?"

9

Squatting on my heels, I said, "I believe I am, Davy. I left nothing behind me, nothing at all."

"Then you won't go to pinin'. A pinin', yearnin' man is no good on the trail. When there's Injuns about, a man keeps his eyes open or he dies . . . an' sometimes he dies, anyway."

He impaled a chunk of meat on a sharpened stick and leaned it over the coals. "You'll need an outfit. Those clothes won't last no time."

"When I shoot some game, I'll make a hunting shirt and leggings."

Davy looked doubtful. "You can do that? Of your ownself?"

"Well, I haven't done it since I was a lad. There was a time when we were very poor. I often made moccasins and once a hunting shirt."

Davy chuckled. "I never seen the time when I wasn't poor." He indicated the sleepers. "They're good men. The long, tall one is Solomon Talley, from Kentuck. Bob Sandy lyin' yonder is from the same neck o' the woods. The stocky, square-shouldered one is Cusbe Ebitt. I never heard him say where he was from, but Degory Kemble is from Virginny, and Isaac Heath is a Boston man."

"What about the Indian?"

"He's an Otoe."

"Known him long?"

"I ain't known none of them long. Deg Kemble an' me, we rafted down to New Orleans, one time. I trapped a season in Winnebago country with Talley. The Otoe comes from the Platte River country . . . knows the river."

One by one, the others drifted to the fire to roast chunks of meat and drink the strong, black coffee.

Heath's eyes kept straying to me, and knowing he was a Boston man, I was ready for the question when it came. "That's an uncommon name you have, my friend."

I shrugged. "Chantry? There've been Chantrys on the frontier for years, Mr. Heath. An ancestor of mine was on the east coast as early as 1602."

My reply was flat and short, spoken with a finality that left small room for questions, and I wanted none. The past was in the past and there I wanted it to remain. If he had been in

Boston within the past few months, he might know that which I wished to forget.

We mounted and rode west with the Otoe scouting ahead, his pony knee-deep in the tall bluestem grasses. Occasionally flocks of prairie chickens flew up, then glided away across the grass to disappear like smoke. Far off we saw several moving black dots.

"Buffalo," Talley said. "We'll be seeing them by the thousand, Chantry. This is their country we're coming to, and a grand, broad country it is."

He leaned down from his saddle and pulled a handful of the bluestem. "Look at it, man! And this is the country some call the Great American Desert! They're fools, Chantry! Fools! Earth that will grow such grass will grow rye or barley or wheat. These plains could feed the world!"

"If you could get men to live on them," Ebitt said wryly. "It's too big for them, too grand. They can't abide the greatness of the sky, or the distances." He pointed ahead. "Look! There's no end yonder. No horizon. You ride on and on and on and all is emptiness. Only the buffalo, the antelope, and the grass bending before the wind. I've seen men frightened by it, Chantry! I've seen them turn tail and run back to their cities and their villages. Only in Russia or the Sahara is there anything like it."

"There's the pampas, on the Argentine," I suggested. "I've not been there, but it must be very like this."

"Maybe," Ebitt said skeptically, "but I think there's nothing like it, not anywhere. The Sahara's desert. Well, Russia, maybe, like I said. I've talked with Russians and there seems to be a vastness to their land as well."

My mind was on other things, for by nature I am a cautious man. "How much does the Otoe understand?" I asked Talley.

"Not much, I'm thinking, but you can't tell about a redskin. They talk little when there's a white man about, but they listen, and nobody in his right mind thinks an Indian is not quick.

"He hasn't our education, and his upbringing isn't Christian, but there's nothing wrong with his senses or his wits. He's tuned to the land, Chantry, and don't ever forget he's lived in this country, in this same way, for a mighty long time."

"Not on the plains," Deg Kemble objected. "Until the Indian got the horse from the white man, he never traveled far over the grassland. He followed streams, and followed the buffalo at times, but there's nothing to live on out here. Once the redskin got the horse, there was no holding him."

Davy Shanagan rode up beside us. "Chantry, I'm cuttin' out to shoot some meat. Want to ride along?"

We turned away from our small column and trotted our horses over the prairie, then walked them to the summit of a small knoll. We found ourselves with a surprising view of the country around.

Within sight, but some distance off, were two herds of antelope, but no buffalo. Far and away to the westward there seemed to be a fold in the hills with some treetops showing.

"There's game along the creeks," Shanagan said. "The Otoe told us that. None of us ever been this far west before. There's bear occasionally, some deer, and lots of prairie chickens."

We walked our horses toward the antelope but holding a course that, while bringing us nearer, seemed aimed at passing them by. At first they seemed unimpressed, but as we continued to advance one or two of them started to move. We decided to have a try at them although they were a good two hundred yards off.

Drawing rein, I lifted the Ferguson to my shoulder, took a careful sight, then squeezed off my shot. The antelope stumbled, then broke into a run. From childhood I had learned to *think* my bullet to the target, for given a chance the eye is accurate, and I knew a deer would sometimes run a quarter of a mile with a bullet through its heart.

The antelope raced on, running swiftly, until suddenly it crumpled, kicked, and lay still.

Davy shot at the instant I did, and his long Kentucky rifle held true. As we rode up to our game, he got out his ramrod and prepared to reload. "Better load up, Chantry. You don't want to be ketched with an empty rifle."

"I am loaded."

He glanced at me, then at the Ferguson, but made no comment. He was a better skinner than I, so while he skinned out both our kills and selected the best cuts of the meat, I kept watch from a nearby knoll.

He was working only a few yards from me and he said, "Can't take nothing for granted. Looks like open country but there's hollows and coulees out yonder where you could hide an army. Just when you figure there ain't anybody within miles, a dozen Injuns come foggin' it out of a coulee and you've lost your hair."

My eyes were getting accustomed to the country. It is remarkable how one's vision becomes limited to nearby objects and what we expect to see. Out here the distance was enormous, a vast sky and an endless rolling plain of grass to which the eye must adjust.

First the mind must accept the clouds, the grass bending before the wind, the changes in the light on the grass, and the shadows left by clouds. Soon the mind has sorted the usual sights and the eye becomes quick to pick up the unusual, the smallest wrong movement in the bend of grass, a deepening of a shadow at the wrong place. The land where I had spent my earliest years was forest and foothills, with frequent streams. Here the only trees were along the watercourses. Later, in New England, I had hunted in farming country, occasionally taking trips into the mountains of Vermont or to Maine. The open plains were new to me, and I was wary of them.

"Known many Indians?"

"Here and there," Davy acknowledged. "Shawnees, mostly. Some Ponca Sioux, Cherokee, and Delaware. I've no bad thought for them. They have their ways and we ours, but when it comes to livin' in this country, their way is best.

"Bob Sandy now, he figures the only good Injun is a dead one. He come home from the mill one time with his pa to find his family butchered, their cabin burned. Even the pigs were shot full of arrows.

"So Bob, he's got a full-sized grudge against Injuns. That's why we put him up to watchin' the Otoe."

"You're watching him? You don't trust him?"

"Chantry, that Injun is ridin' toward his own people. What we got may seem mighty small to a gent from back east, but to an Injun, it's treasure. If he could murder us all, or set a trap with his own folks to kill us, they'd have all we got and he'd be a big man among his own folks.

"They got no Christian upbringin'. Nobody ever told them to forgive their enemies, or told them that stealin' was bad, except in their own village, from their own people. With most Injuns the word stranger is the same as that for enemy.

"A lot of white men think the Injun is dead set against them because they're white. Nothing to it. An Injun will kill another Injun as quick as he will a white man, except that the white man may have more loot on him."

"They've had it pretty good, Davy. The best hunting in the world, no taxes to pay, and a lot of country to move around in."

"Uh-huh"—Shanagan chuckled—"that's your Boston showin'. What you don't figure on is that you folks yonder in civilization have yourselves nicely protected by the law and custom. Out here you've got no protection but a quick eye, a fast horse, and the ability to shoot straight.

"That free savage that folks talk about, he never leaves his camp but what somebody is likely to take his hair."

After that neither of us spoke for some time. My own thoughts strayed far afield. These broad plains must resemble those from which the wild riding Scythians migrated when they moved west and south from Central Asia. They took scalps as well, although they worked with metal and were in many ways further advanced than the American Indian.

Out of Central Asia our own people had come . . . or perhaps from the lands east of the Danube or Don. The question is disputed, but my own inclination is toward Central Asia. Among those migrating tribes were the Celts and we who moved farthest to the west, we Irish, Welsh, and Bretons, still kept some of the old beliefs, the old customs.

Since the beginning of time, men had been migrating, with the movement usually to the south or west. Perhaps this of which I was now a part would be the last great migration. Yet this was different. This was no organized movement of tribes, nations, or conquering armies; it was a migration of individuals, each making his own decision, gathering his own supplies and equipment. From a thousand villages and cities they came, strangers to each other, yet with a common goal.

Over the mountains from the coastal provinces, filtering down the slopes, floating down the rivers, some dying, some living, many killed by savages, but the dead were always replaced by others. There was no end to them.

I had seen them on the Monongahela and the Ohio, floating their rafts downstream, finding homes in Illinois, Missouri, or going on to Texas.

Here and there I heard talk of Oregon, and of California. Once a man has made that first move, once he has cast off his moorings, his associations, broken with his school, his church, his village store, and his relatives, it is easy to continue on. It is always easier to travel than to stop.

As long as one travels toward a promised land, the dream is there, to stop means to face the reality, and it is easier to dream than to realize the dream.

"You spoke of the Injuns awhile back, their hunting, and all. Hunting is all right when there's game, but the game drifts when the climate changes, and during the winter there's no berries or nuts or seeds to be had, so grub can be mighty hard to come by."

"You're right, of course. But they did smoke meat, and some of the Indians planted corn and squash."

"You bet they did, but Injuns aren't much hand to put by. I lived among 'em a time or two when their bellies were empty and the papooses cried themselves to sleep. It took a lot of grub to get them through the winter, and I reckon no tribe ever had enough."

Remembering my own early years, I could only agree. Many a time before I had the Ferguson rifle, we had gone hungry, and there'd been a few times after. More than once I'd hiked miles through the wet woods hunting something when all the animals had laid up to wait out the storm.

Suddenly, Shanagan pulled up, pointing. The tracks of several riders of unshod ponies had passed diagonally across our route, and not long since. They had drawn up here, watching our party go by.

"We'd better be gettin' back." Davy took a look around, then we raced our horses across the flat to get back to the others. Solomon Talley rode to meet us.

"They heard our shootin'," Davy said. "They could never have missed it, but they didn't attack even when they knew our guns were empty."

Cusbe Ebitt spat. "They want us all together, and at the right time."

"Likely," Heath agreed. He glanced at the antelope. "Two shots, two kills. That's prime!"

"Don't worry none about Chantry," Shanagan told them. "His was a runnin' shot, two hundred yards if an inch, and right through the heart."

We spread out to offer less of a target, yet you could have drawn a fifty-yard circle around the lot of us. Back east there was much talk of the red man and the wrongs that had been done him, but I found myself less concerned with those wrongs and more with my own scalp at this moment.

"You got to see it their way," Davy said. "To an Injun our outfit would make him a mighty rich man. One ambush, and they ride home loaded with powder, shot, traps, blankets, rifles, and horses, to say nothing of our trifles."

Ahead of us was a knoll where a fringe of woodland came up out of a stream bed and crested the knoll. There were a few granite boulders around.

We spread out into a skirmish line and rode up the slope. There was a spring flowing from under a boulder, several cottonwood trees, and one huge fallen one. There was a little brush.

Only the Otoe hung back. "No good," he said. "Bad spirits here."

"Looks all right to me," Bob Sandy said.

We walked our horses into the little hollow atop the knoll. On our north side, the ground fell steeply away into a coulee where our spring's water trickled away to join a small stream.

A more perfect camping place could not be found, but no ashes of campfires existed. There were many evidences of antelope, buffalo, and even wild horses about, and no bones to indicate a poison spring. Such springs were rare, but I had heard of some with arsenic in the water, and others with numerous minerals in suspension that might upset the human organism.

Talley swung down and tasted the water. "Hell, there's nothing wrong with that. I never tasted better."

"No good," the Otoe insisted. He gestured sweepingly. "No like. Bad place for Indian."

Deg Kemble prowled about while Ebitt rode out along the ridge above the stream. On all three .sides but that of the stream we would have an excellent field of fire with protection from a natural mound of earth that banked the source of the spring on three sides. On the other the fallen log offered an equally fine breastwork. The space within was perhaps thirty yards by twenty, ample for ourselves and our horses.

The Otoe hung back. Obviously he wanted no part of the place.

Talley stopped by where I still sat my horse. "You are an educated man, Chantry. What do you make of him?"

"There seem to be two possibilities. One that he didn't intend to bring us here because the place is too good a position to defend, in case he's planned to ambush us, or else the place is taboo for some reason."

"Taboo?"

"An Indian doesn't have our knowledge, and for what he cannot otherwise explain, he imagines evil spirits are the cause. For example, suppose some Indians got hold of the blankets or clothing of people who died by smallpox and rode to this place with them. As you know, such things have happened and the Indians died very quickly.

"Other Indians may have found the bodies, dead but with no marks upon them, and would immediately assume evil spirits had been at work. After all, Kemble, it's only a few years since we were doing the same thing."

"Makes sense. Anyway, I'm for stayin'. You agree?"

"I do."

Later I wondered if my advice was sound. No one among us was the leader. Each had his abilities, each contributed in his own way.

While I put together a small fire, Isaac Heath picketed the horses, Bob Sandy and the Otoe kept watch, Shanagan staked out our antelope hides and began scraping them of excess flesh.

The others gathered fuel for the night and Cusbe Ebitt put on a kettle and began to prepare a stew.

Talley went off down the trickle to the stream, scouting the country.

My fire going, I went to the edge and looked out over the vastness of the prairie, the grass flame red with the setting sun. For the first time, I realized what a move I had made.

My wife and child were gone. Burned to death in the flames of a fire set by . . . *whom?*

Or was it purely accident, like so many others? Sudden fires were not uncommon.

But what had *I* done? I had cut all ties, abandoned the planning of a lifetime, and ridden off into a wild land. Only two months ago I had sat with distinguished men, men of letters, directors of affairs, leaders of men, and now here I was, far off in the wilderness headed toward what?

THREE

The sky was shot with flaming arrows that slowly faded, leaving a kiss of crimson on the edges of clouds, and the prairie itself turned a sullen red, darkening into shadows and the night. Somewhere down in the copse an owl hooted.

It was an empty land, but I knew my people, and it would not be empty long. I had seen them back there with their simple wagons. I had seen them afoot, with wife and child riding, sometimes driving a cow, crossing the mountains, clearing the roads.

Already they had cut paths into the dark forests of Pennsylvania and Ohio. Men had long been trapping west of the Mississippi as well as east of it, and the adventurous ones, such as this party, were pushing out into the plains.

Those families crossing the mountains carried their axes and shovels . . . they would not be stopped. Where there was land to be taken, they would go, and then they would grow restless and rise up and move westward again and again.

Turning back toward the fire I was stopped by Heath's voice: ". . . killed a man in a duel. The man said something about Chantry settin' the fire himself, an' Chantry challenged him.

19

The fellow was a loudmouth, just blowing off with a lot of loose talk. He tried to back out, but Chantry wouldn't let him. Told him to make his fight or he'd shoot him like the dog he was. The man fought. Chantry let him shoot first, and the bullet burned Chantry's neck . . . drew blood. Then Chantry shot him."

"Kill him?"

"That he did, and d'you know where the bullet hit him?"

"In the mouth," Solomon Talley said. "He shot him in the mouth."

Heath turned on him. "You've heard the story, then?"

"No," Talley replied grimly, "but that's a hard man yonder. Besides," he added, "that's what I'd o' done."

For a few minutes I stood silent, letting the talk turn to other things, and then I started forward, making enough noise so they would know I was nearby.

They knew then, and I wished they did not. There are times when to be just nobody at all is the best thing. All that was past I wanted to forget.

For in a sense I was running away, not only from the scenes of love and happiness turned to grief, but from the whispered stories that implied I myself had started the fire that killed all I loved. Such a rumor starts easily, but how to put it down?

Nor did I wish to be pitied or to find doors closing in my face that had once been open to me.

My hands held the Ferguson rifle. In the months and years to come, it might be all there would ever be. It was mine. Not only that, but it reminded me of my mother, of our old cabin where we had been hungry yet rich in love, of my wife, who often rode to the hunt with me, and of my son whom I had taught to shoot with this very rifle.

Walking up to the fire, I squatted beside it, wiping my hatband with my fingers. "The sky says it will be windy tomorrow," I said.

"Aye," Ebitt agreed. "There's stew, man. You'd best finish it off so's we can clean the kettle. And you'll be needin' some coffee."

There was talk then by the campfire, the good talk of

frontiersmen, and I listened for I had much to learn. I had studied at the Sorbonne and at Heidelberg and I had taught history at Cambridge and William and Mary but what I had to learn from these men could be found in no book. They had been early upon the land, hunting and trapping for their living, and they knew well the land to which I had but lately come.

Firelight danced upon their faces. There was the good smell of a wood fire burning, of coffee freshly made, and the smell of meat broiling, and of the stew.

Something had happened during the day, for I had killed game, brought meat to the fire. They knew now that I was no drone, and that in whatever came I would carry my weight.

They were hard men living upon a hard land that demanded much, and the fact that I had killed an enemy in a face-to-face meeting meant something to them. It was a thing they understood. In the east, where duels occurred frequently, but were already looked upon with distaste in some quarters, this was not always the case.

Solomon Talley accepted the first watch, and Isaac Heath volunteered for the second. As for me, I requested the final watch, knowing Indians preferred attacks by daybreak.

Again I saw the Otoe's eyes upon my rifle, and I smiled at him. He did not respond, but looked away. Already I was tired. My body had not accustomed itself to the long hours of riding, and I wished to be fresh for my guard duty, so I opened my small blanket roll and went to sleep.

Hours later I was gently awakened. It was Heath. "Come, man, it's three by the clock, and a night with stars."

Rolling out, I folded my bed, tugged on my boots, and slipped into my jacket. Heath looked at me and shook his head. "Those brass buttons now, they make a fair mark for shooting."

"I know that. I'll risk it until I can make a shirt. Has it been quiet?"

Heath shrugged. "Yes, if you can call it that. Frogs down below, and the usual coyotes, but the light is deceitful. You'll have to keep a wary eye for trouble."

Taking my rifle, I went out to the perimeter of the knoll and looked down over the prairie below. All seemed to be empty and still. In the darkness a good bit was yet visible, and I walked slowly, halfway around the camp, then quickly doubled back and came around from the opposite direction.

Heath added a few small chunks to the fire to keep the coals alive for morning, then turned in.

The camp was still. If an attack was to come, the obvious place was from out of the creek bed where nothing could be seen. One by one I checked off the sleeping positions of my friends. Talley, Ebitt, Sandy, Kemble, Shanagan, Heath, and the Otoe.

The time drew on, and my ears became attuned to the night. I moved off, never circling the same way twice, never completing a circle, for I wished to establish no pattern, no way I could be timed. In the far-off east there seemed to be a lightening of the sky, but it was early for that.

For several minutes I was conscious of something wrong before it occurred to me that the frogs had ceased their endless croaking. The night was suddenly silent.

Near a boulder I squatted, one toe slightly behind the other, listening.

Nothing . . . no sound.

I turned my head. Should I awaken them? I did not want to make them lose their sleep because of my own foolishness. I could awaken one of them . . . Talley, perhaps.

Talley . . . Ebitt . . . Sandy . . . Kemble . . . Davy Shanagan, Isaac Heath, and the—

The Otoe was gone!

Horses . . . first they would stampede the horses. That much I had learned. Swiftly, I ran to them. They were nervous, heads up, nostrils distended.

"Shanagan," I said.

And a shadow moved . . . a horse snorted, and I sidestepped as a darker shadow lunged toward me. There was the gleam of firelight on a knifeblade, and I chopped, short and hard, with the butt of my rifle.

He was coming low and fast and the butt *thunked* against his skull and he went down hard. Turning swiftly as another came in over the low mound, I fired.

My shot was from the hip, for there was no chance to aim. It caught the Indian and turned him but my hands went automatically for bullet and powder.

All was suddenly still. Unused to combat, I had expected the clash of arms, the scream of wounded, the stabbing flames of shooting . . . and there was nothing.

Stepping back among the horses, I went from one to the other, whispering to quiet them down. From where I stood, I could see the beds of the others, all empty.

Something stirred near me and I turned swiftly. Davy's voice was scarcely breathed. "You all right?"

"The Otoe was gone. I went to the horses, thinking they might try to stampede them."

"You done right." He could see the body on the ground about a dozen feet away. "You got one?"

"Two, I think. I shot one over there."

I started forward and Shanagan caught my arm. "Uh-uh. They'll still be out there."

There was a faint lemon tinge to the far-off sky now. We stood waiting, listening.

An owl hooted . . . inquiringly. After a bit, the same owl.

Davy's lips at my ear whispered, "Wonderin' where this one is."

The sky lightened, red streaks shot up, and high in the heavens a cloud blushed faintly at the earth below.

We waited, not moving, not knowing what might come. The Indians might press the attack, might draw away to wait for a better moment. The red man is under no compulsion to continue a fight. He does not insist upon victory at any cost, and he has time. He is under no compulsion to win *now*.

Now the sky brightened quickly. We moved to the perimeter, seeking firing positions. The plain below was innocent of life.

Degory Kemble moved over to us. "There's nobody in sight," he said. "My guess is they've pulled out." He saw the Indian lying in the dust and moved over to him. With his toe he turned him over, holding his rifle ready for a shot if the warrior proved to be playing possum.

He was quite dead. One side of his head was bloody, crushed by my blow. I turned away, and looked out over the prairie.

"You want his hair?" Davy asked. "He's yours."

"No," I said. "It's a barbaric custom."

"This here is a barbaric land. You get yourself a few scalps and the Injuns will respect you more."

"Take it if you wish."

"No. By rights it's yours."

Kemble carefully broke the dead warrior's arrows, then his bow. His knife he tossed to me and that I kept. "Trade it for something," Kemble said. "It's worth a good beaver pelt."

"I thought I shot one," I said. "He came in right over there."

"They're like prairie dogs," Talley commented. "If you don't kill them right dead, they're gone into some hole."

We walked over to where I'd seen the Indian, and suddenly Talley pointed. "Hit him, all right. See yonder?"

There was a spot of blood, very red, splashed upon a leaf. Just beyond we found two more.

We followed no farther for the trail of blood vanished into thick brush, and he might be lying down there, waiting for us.

"Lung shot, I'd say," Kemble said. "You nailed him proper." He looked at me. "For a pilgrim, you sure take hold. That's as good shootin' as a man can do."

"I didn't want to kill him," I said. Then I paused. That was not quite true, because I certainly had not wanted him to kill me, and it was one or the other.

"If you'd not shot him, he'd have thought you a coward or a poor warrior. He'd despise you for it. You better think this through because there ain't no two ways about it. You got to be ready to shoot to kill or you better go back home."

He was right, of course, and had not men always fought? We walked back to the fire where coffee was on. Bob Sandy came in. He had gone stalking and found nothing.

"They pulled out," he said regretfully. "They're no fools. The Otoe probably figured with a tenderfoot on watch it would be easy." He grinned at me. "You fooled 'em, you surely did."

"I was fortunate," I said, "and scared."

"You bet you was," Sandy said, "an' you better stay scared.

Time comes you stop bein' scared, you better go back east, because you won't last long after."

We sat around the fire and ate, and looking around at their faces, I thought of Homer and the Greeks camped on the shore waiting to advance on Troy.

These were men of the same kind, men of action, fighting men, no better and no worse than those.

FOUR

N othing anyone can say can tell you how it was upon that land of grass. Horizon to horizon, upon every side, it stretched to infinity, and overhead the enormous vault of the sky.

We plodded westward, and the land unrolled before us. More and more, as we moved away from the settlements, there was wild game, the buffalo in increasing numbers, and antelope often in herds of sixty or seventy.

At streams where we stopped for water, we often found the tracks of bear, occasionally of lion. Wolves and the small prairie wolf called the coyote lurked in the vicinity of the buffalo, watching for a chance to pick off a calf or one too old to put up much of a fight.

We rode warily, for there was no security even upon the open plains, because such openness was only seeming and not a reality. My boyhood became important, for then my eye had developed a quickness that became useful once more, and I was swift to perceive any unexpected and unnatural motion. My attention soon became adjusted to wind movements in the grass so that I would quickly note any other. Yet I looked for other things as well, for the scholar in me would not yield.

For some time, being a student of history, I had been excited by the influence of climate upon history, and especially upon the movements of peoples. The sudden appearance of the Huns or the Goths in Europe, for example, and the earlier migrations of Celtic peoples . . . what occasioned these moves? Was it the pressure of other tribes, increasing in numbers? Or was it drought? Or the ever-present movement toward the sun?

Several times we saw the tracks of unshod ponies, and from their direction and purposeful movement, it was easy to see they were not wild ponies, but ridden by Indians. During this time, I began to see that in the Ferguson rifle I possessed a kind of insurance the others did not have.

Also I was having second thoughts about my clothing. I must have something more fitting for travel, but instead of discarding the clothes I wore, I must keep them for use on ceremonial occasions. The American Indian, I recalled, was ever a man of dignity, with a love of formality, and it behooved me to approach him in a like manner.

The Otoe was gone, departed with his friends whom he had invited to the raid. I was still astonished at the suddenness of it, and the equally abrupt end. I had expected more.

Since the beginning of time, men have been moving into empty spaces, and we in America were no different than those others, the Goths, the Mongols, the Indo-Aryans. We were but the last of the great migrations, and I wondered as I rode . . . how much choice did we really have? Plants move rapidly into areas for which they are best adapted, and human migrations seem to follow the same principles.

For three days we rode westward, and we left behind the long grasses. Not yet had we reached the shortgrass country that lay still farther west. The tall bluestem we had seen on previous days now disappeared except in the bottoms along the creeks. Judging by the grass, the climate was hotter, and much drier . . . wheatgrass, little bluestem and occasionally patches of buffalo grass and blue grama.

This land must have seen few Indians until the arrival of the horse, for the distances were great and water was increasingly scarce.

We rode to the Platte for water. The riverbed was wide and sandy, the river itself was shallow, and the water somewhat brackish. We drank, then rode back from the river and camped in a small cluster of trees on rising ground with a good field of fire in all directions.

While the others made camp and Sandy went with Heath to graze the horses, I cut out my hunting jacket and a pair of leggings. The buckskin was not properly prepared, nearly impossible to do while on the march. At home there had been a smooth log over which to throw the skin when scraping away the fat and membrane. On the trail I had to make do as best I could with what offered. Nor could I soak the hide in water and wood ashes for three days or so. I did put the hide to soak each time we made camp, and then scraped the hair loose as best I could. We had kept the brains of the antelope and these had been dried. Now I stewed them with some fat and rubbed the mixture into the hide. When that was completed, I stretched the hide and then rolled it carefully to keep for a couple of days longer before I finished it with scraping and smoking.

This was done by Indian women in the villages, but I must do it myself or go without, and I wished to save what clothing I had for those special occasions. The life of the Indian, whether man or woman, was never easy. To subsist in wild country called for much work, and for the squaws at least it was an unceasing task.

Degory Kemble rode into camp just as the sun had set, bringing with him the best cuts of meat from a buffalo calf.

When he was squatted by the fire, gnawing on a bone, he glanced up. "I saw something yonder," he said, "that shapes up for trouble."

We waited, looking at him. He chewed for a moment, then said, "Moccasin tracks . . . boots among 'em. Maybe three white men, Spanish men, I'd say."

"What's that to us?" Heath asked.

"They don't look kindly on folks coming into their neighborhood," Talley explained. "Bonaparte sort of took Louisiana from the Spanish, then sold it to us. The Spanish have a settlement or two down yonder and they throw anybody into prison who comes into their country." He swept a hand in a wide arc. "They claim most of this here, an' nobody ever did decide rightly where the boundary was. I heard of some French soldiers in Colorado . . . hunting gold. The Spanish set the Utes on them."

"Then we had best be careful," I suggested. "Do you think they've seen us?"

"Doubt it," Kemble commented, "but there's a big party, maybe forty in all. One of them might have hunted far enough east to see us."

We ate in silence, for there was much to think about. We were far from others of our kind, and could expect no help if trouble developed. The Spanish and the Indians had villages not too far off, but we were seven men alone, as if on another planet.

Yet there is a strength implicit in such a situation, for having no one on which to rely, we relied upon no one. Our problem was our own, and what must be done we would do ourselves, and looking about me, I decided that had I selected each man, I could have done no better.

These men were typical of what I had seen among those floating down the Ohio, crossing the Alleghenies or the Appalachians, coming west by whatever means . . . they were men who had chosen themselves. Each in his own mind had made the decision to go west. No king, no queen or general or president had said "Go west," but each man in his own way had decided, and finding what they faced had not turned back.

Looking upon these men, I knew that I, who had attended lectures at the Sorbonne and Heidelberg, who had himself lectured at Cambridge and William and Mary, I who had lunched with President Jefferson, who was a friend to Captain Meriwether Lewis, Henry Dearborn, Dr. William Thornton, Gilbert Stuart, and Count de Volney, I had at last come home. These were my people, this was my country.

Isaac Heath turned his head to me. "Is that true, Chantry? Is there no border?"

"None has been defined. That's one reason for the Lewis and Clark expedition. Not only to see what lies out there, but to establish our presence in the area."

Davy Shanagan appeared at the edge of the firelight. "Somebody comin'," he said softly. "Five or six, maybe."

His words were spoken over an empty fire, for each of us vanished ghostlike into the surrounding darkness. I, fortunately, had the presence of mind to retain my coffee. With the Ferguson rifle in my right hand, I drank coffee from the cup in my left.

A voice called out . . . in Spanish, and I replied in the same tongue, stepping quickly to the right as I did so. No shot was fired, and we heard the riders coming nearer. Two Spanish men, and four Indians.

Stepping into the firelight, I invited them to dismount. They did so, striding up to the fire. The man in the lead looked at me coolly. "I'm Captain Luis Fernandez!" he said. "I'm an officer of Spain."

I bowed slightly. I could see he was somewhat surprised at my garb. "It's a pleasure to meet you, senor," I replied, "so far from home. On behalf of the American people, I welcome you to our country."

There was nothing to be lost, I decided, in landing the first blow. That he was shocked was obvious. "*Your* country?" he exclaimed indignantly. "But this is Spanish territory!"

The others of my party moved from the shadows, all except Shanagan and Bob Sandy, who wisely remained on watch.

"Will you join us in some coffee, captain?" I suggested. Then I added, "I wasn't aware that your king's claims extended so far. In any event, the Louisiana Territory has been sold to the United States by the Emperor Napoleon."

He stared at me in total disbelief. Yet my assurance left him somewhat uncertain, as he accepted the coffee. Glancing from one to the other of us, he suddenly burst out, "I don't believe it! It's impossible!"

"It's true," I replied, and then added, "Under other conditions, captain, I'd resent your disbelief, but I'll overlook it under the circumstances."

Before he could continue, I went on. "By the secret Treaty of San Ildefonso, the territory was returned to France. My government learned of this and began negotiations with the emperor. As you know, the slave revolt in Haiti and impending

war with England left him in need of funds. The Senate approved
the treaty and on the twentieth of December 1803, my government took formal possession.

"To repeat, Captain Fernandez, we welcome you as our
guest."

His face flushed with irritation. Ebitt was grinning openly,
and both Kemble and Talley had difficulty in restraining their
amusement.

"Nonsense!" he exploded, then added quickly, "In any event,
this isn't a part of the Louisiana Territory. It's administered
from Santa Fe."

"I understand your surprise, captain," I replied gently. "In
such wide open country, one often rides farther than one
realizes, but you're now well within the territory of the United
States."

The captain was not pleased. He had come, I was sure, to
order us out of the country or to place us under arrest. Com-
munication was slow and must come by sailing ship from Spain
to Mexico, from Mexico City to Santa Fe, and no doubt Fernandez had been absent several weeks.

"I believe none of this," he said sharply, "and in any event,
you're under arrest. You'll be taken to Santa Fe where your
case will be disposed of . . . in due time."

I smiled at him. "Under arrest, captain? I could as easily
arrest you, but the offense is trivial. I'm sure the amount of
grass your horses have eaten will not cause us to suffer too
much, but as for arresting us, you cannot. And captain, we will
not be arrested."

He threw his cup to the ground. "You'll surrender, or be
taken by force!"

"Take us, then." Solomon Talley spoke quietly. "Take us,
captain."

"I have forty men!" Fernandez threatened. "Surrender at
once or we'll kill you all!"

I smiled at him, then glanced at Kemble and Talley. "Forty?
The number won't divide evenly, Kemble, so I guess it will be
first come, first served."

"I'll get my share," Ebitt said.

Fernandez turned abruptly and strode to his horse. The

others had said nothing, but as he turned to go, one of them lifted a pistol.

"I wouldn't," Heath warned, his rifle on its target. "I just wouldn't at all."

The pistol was lowered, slowly, carefully. Then they rode away into the darkness.

"I hate to leave such a good camp," I said.

"*Leave* it? You don't figure on runnin'?" Ebitt demanded.

"No, I don't. Right yonder"—I pointed back of us—"about forty yards back there's a few big, old cottonwood deadfalls. They fell just right for a breastwork. I ran upon it while I was gathering firewood.

"There're several living trees, and there's room inside for ourselves and our horses, a kind of natural fort. I think it might be wise to leave our fire burning and just pull back."

We did just that, and at the lower end of our natural redoubt, we found the ground fell away slightly in an area where the thick branches of two trees met. There was room enough to hide our horses there, out of sight and safe from stray bullets. In a matter of minutes, we had moved, added fresh fuel to our fire, and settled down behind our breastwork.

"Better get some sleep," Talley advised. "I'll stand watch."

The advice was good and we accepted it, stretching out on the ground. It was thickly bedded with leaves from the fallen trees and those that leaned above us, and we were soon asleep.

Just before I fell finally asleep, I heard Ebitt saying to Kemble, "I never knowed all that about treaties and such. I heard about the purchase . . . that's why I left Illinois to come west. How'd he know all that?"

"Comes of being a scholar," Kemble said.

And we all went to sleep.

FIVE

Awakening in the chill of the hour before dawn, I lay quite still looking up at the stars. At this hour, the sky seems unnaturally clear, and the stars close above. For a moment, lying there, I thought about all that I had seen and much that I had learned from the talk of the men with whom I traveled.

The mind that is geared to learning, that is endlessly curious, cannot cease from contemplating and comparing. To many the grasslands over which we had been riding were simply that, but for me there was much to see, much to learn. No doubt the Indian knew all I was learning, and accepted it as a simple facet of his world.

The tall grass we had left needed moisture, and no doubt during dry years it fell back toward the east with its rivers and its greater rainfall. Then the low-growing grasses invaded, took over, and retained a hold on the earth until once more the wet years brought back the tall bluestem and its companions of the soil.

The buffalo grazed wherever there was grass, into Georgia, Pennsylvania, Kentucky, and Tennessee, but they seemed to like the open country best, out where the long wind blew and the sun was hot upon the low rolling hills.

A whisper snapped me to attention. It was Shanagan. "I believe we're to have comp'ny," he said softly.

Rolling out, I swiftly brought my blankets together, tied them into a neat bundle, and took them to my saddle. My Ferguson was under my arm, but I hastily completed dressing by pulling on my boots and hitching my knife into its proper place.

Our fire had burned low. I could see the red glow of the coals lying just over there. Around me there were furtive stirrings as the others took their places.

Yet when it came we were startled, for they came with a rush and wild warwhoops intended to frighten and demoralize. That such an attack out of the night would have that effect was beyond question, for ready as we were, it was a shock to hear them.

They rushed into the camp, and as one man, we fired. At least two Indians dropped. I think there were more, but in the vague light and with surrounding trees and brush, it was difficult to see.

My own rifle was almost instantly loaded, yet I held my fire a moment to give the others a start on reloading, not wanting all to be empty at once. Shanagan fired his pistol, and then I fired and instantly reloaded . . . and then there were no targets.

The attackers had vanished as swiftly as they had come.

A body or two lay sprawled near our fire, but that was all, and there was no sound.

The sky was turning gray, with a faint touch of lemon light along the eastern horizon, and far above us a wisp of cloud blushed faintly.

We waited behind our fallen timber, watching the light grow. Slowly the blackness took on shape and form, the shapes became trees, bushes, and rocks, and on the ground a dead Indian. From under the bushes, I saw the feet of another.

Still we waited, and as the light grew, we could see the plain was empty of life. At last Degory Kemble came out from the redoubt and went to the nearest of the fallen Indians.

"Ute," he said. "This is far north for them. Mostly they're mountain Indians."

"From Spanish country?" I asked.

"They claim it, but so did the French. I figure it for the Louisiana Territory. The border should be south of there."

"It will need some time to decide that," I said.

"And meanwhile?"

"We'll hunt there, and trap for beaver, although it would be better for all of us if we could establish relations with Santa Fe. They need the trade and so do we."

"They're a long way from Mexico City," Talley agreed. "Saint Louis is closer."

One by one we emerged and scouted our small patch of woods. No Indians were left. We found a spot of blood or two that seemed to indicate a wound, and a dropped rifle of Spanish make. One of the dead Indians had an old musket; the other had been armed with a bow and arrows.

We wasted no time, but packed our horses and moved out, leaving the Indians as they were. Bob Sandy took the scalps for himself. Talley rode point, Kemble twenty yards to the left, and I an equal distance to the right. Ebitt and Sandy followed Kemble and me at about ten yards' distance, with Heath and Shanagan to bring up the rear.

We presented no good target, yet had a chance to scout the country as we rode. We started at a walk, moving to a trot after a few hundred yards, holding it for some distance.

Except for my own, our horses were prairie-bred mustangs and they held the pace easily. My horse was of better breed but lacked the staying quality of the once wild horses, and was accustomed to better feed.

It was obvious that my horse must adjust to the change in diet and traveling conditions or I must find another one. In time, if allowed to run free, he might fit himself to the country . . . as I must do also.

Physically my condition had never been bad, and my muscles and skin were hardening to the work. Mentally it was another story. I had fought when attacked, acquitting myself well, and I believe those with whom I traveled believed me adequate for the journey before us. Such was not the case.

As a matter of fact, I had no stomach for killing. I considered myself a reasonably civilized man, and killing was wrong. Nor did I decide this by simple biblical standards, for the Bible, Hebrew scholars had assured me, did not say, "Thou shalt not kill," but strictly interpreted it says, "Thou shalt not commit murder," which is quite another thing.

Yet it was not the Mosaic law that guided me, but my own intelligence. I had no right to deprive another human being of his life, nor had I the intention of adding to the violence that was around me. On the other hand, the Indians I had killed would surely have killed me had I not been more fortunate than they.

Nevertheless, the destruction of the Indians did not please me, and I hoped to avoid it in the future.

The problem was that I was a civilized man, but I now existed in an uncivilized world. The standards by which I thought were standards of the ordered world I had left behind. Much had been said in both England and our own eastern states about how we treated the "poor" Indian.

The few I had seen on the plains did not look poor. They were strong, able men . . . warriors.

Warriors.

That was the key word. These men did not consider themselves *poor*. They were proud men, carrying their heads high, walking tall, the equal of any man. What they demanded was not pity, but respect. The problem was that two kinds of men had now come face-to-face, two kinds of men with two kinds of standards, different scruples, different responses.

Being a civilized, cultured human being was all very well, but I must hedge my bets a little or I would be a dead civilized, cultured human being.

It needs two to make a peace, but only one to make an attack.

Humanity, I decided, must be tempered with reason, and reason with reality.

I said as much to Solomon Talley. He glanced at me and I am afraid he was amused. "I'm no scholar, Chantry, and I've done no reasoning on the question. The first time an Indian notched an arrow at me, I shot him, and I'm almighty pleased that I hit him."

And so it was they began calling me by the name that was to

stick through many years. I was no longer Ronan Chantry except at intervals. I became known as Scholar.

Part of it was gentle derision, but another part was, I think, respect.

One thing I learned quickly, in those following weeks. The university of the wilderness that I now attended had simple tests but they came often. One lived if one passed the tests, but to get a failing grade was to leave one's scalp on some brave's belt.

On Talley's advice we deviated from our planned course and angled off to the north, taking us farther from the disputed territory, and we held to low ground, trying to keep our route unknown to the enemy. For we had no doubt that Captain Fernandez and his Indian allies would be observing us and planning another attack. Nor could we hope to be so successful again. The captain, although our enemy, was no fool. Any officer in his situation might easily have overrated his strength and our cunning. Both he and his Indian friends now knew us better.

Where *were* the mountains? They lay somewhere to the westward, but not one of us had seen them, and the endlessness of the plains was beyond belief. The land was higher now, and much drier. We had come into the shortgrass country, and the prickly pear we had originally come upon from time to time now were frequent.

Water was scarce. Many of the streams were dry, the waterholes only trampled mud. Then suddenly we saw the buffalo.

First there was the sound of them, a low, shuffling sound that we thought was the wind, yet a strange, muffled muttering as well. We topped the rise, and they were before us, thousands upon thousands of them, grazing and moving.

"Hold your fire," I suggested to the others. "I can reload and we'll kill just two."

"What about the hides? Ain't they worth something?"

"A buffalo hide, at least the hide of a bull, will weigh nigh to fifty pounds. We're in no shape to pack them."

While the others held their fire in the event our enemies

were near, I rode forward, dismounted near a rock, and using a shoulder of it for a rest, killed two buffalo.

The others seemed not to notice, yet when we rode down to cut up our kill, they moved off.

And then I saw the Indians.

They were several hundred yards off and had been approaching the buffalo from the other flank, the wind, light as it was, being due out of the north. I saw an Indian rise suddenly from the ground and throw off a buffalo robe. Using it as cover, he had been slowly creeping up to the herd to make a kill, and our moving up had caused him to lose his chance. His disgust was obvious.

Heath and Sandy were on the ground, making the cuts to skin the buffalo and cut out the meat.

"Somethin' odd here," Talley muttered. "There's ten to twelve women there, and a bunch of kids, but there don't seem to be more than one or two braves . . . and no ponies."

"They've been raided," Shanagan said. "Bet my shirt on it. Somebody drove off their stock and either killed the menfolk or the braves are off tryin' to get back their horses."

"What are they? Can you make them out?"

"Cheyennes," Davy said positively. "I'd swear they were Cheyennes, some of the bravest and best fighters on the plains."

"Talley," I said, "if we're going to live in this country, we'll need friends, and if we're going to have friends, now's a chance to meet them."

"I can talk a little sign language," Shanagan said. "What's your idea?"

"Give them the hides," I said, "and half the meat."

"We can take our cuts," Talley said. "They'll eat everything but the horns."

Hand high, palm outward, I rode toward them, with Davy beside me. The hunter had returned to the others, and as we drew near, they waited. There was only one warrior among them able to stand. Two young boys and an old man were all that was left aside from the women and children.

"I come as a friend," I said, and Davy translated, using sign talk. "We are strong in war, and we have hunted. We would share our meat with our friends."

Now that we were closer we could see the hunger among them. Another brave, whom we had not seen, was stretched on a travois, obviously badly wounded.

Talley came riding up. "We've taken our meat," he said. "Let 'em have what's left."

They followed us to the two buffalo and at once began butchering their remains. The one strong brave remained near us, watching but still wary.

"Ask him what happened," I suggested.

Davy went to work, and the warrior told the story swiftly and in sign talk. I marveled at the gracefulness of the gestures, the ease and poetry of the hand movements.

"During the last full moon, some Utes hit them. Killed four braves and three women, drove off their horses, and would have killed them all, but they fought them to a standstill.

"The Utes pulled off, taking their horses along. Eight of their braves left alive followed to try to steal the horses back. Since then, they've had one antelope, wild onions, and that's about all."

"Last full moon?" Ebitt muttered. "That's close on to three weeks."

Soon we had found a camping place in a hollow near a slough. Within minutes the Indians were roasting the meat, some of them eating it raw. They were an attractive people, with strongly cut, regular features and fine physiques.

True to my nature I had taken the time to study what was known about the western Indians as well as the country itself. Much was supposition, but James Mooney had gathered for the Bureau of Ethnology estimates on the various tribes. In 1780 the Cheyennes numbered about thirty-five hundred . . . which would figure out to some seven or eight hundred warriors, although it might be much less.

I said as much to Talley. "That could be right," he commented, "although you rarely see many in a bunch. The country won't support them, so they split up into small bands like this.

"That's why they keep moving. The game drifts away from their villages and soon they've collected all the roots, seeds, and berries there are to be had. We feed several hundred people on land that will support maybe one Indian family."

"Talley," I suggested, "these Indians need help, and we can use the company. Why don't we stay with them if they're going our way?"

"All right," Talley said. "I figure it was that same party who attacked us who stole their horses. There aren't apt to be two bands of Utes this far from their home country."

The warrior had come over to where we sat our horses, Shanagan with him. "He's worried," Davy said. "His folks should have been back."

"Tell him his people need meat. We will stay until his young men return if they move west with us."

Davy's fingers grew busy, and the reply came quickly, on the brave's eloquent fingers. "They're going west, and he thanks you."

What would my friend Timothy Dwight think of me now? Riding west with a band of Indians?

Remembering the man, and what he knew of me, I smiled, for he would not have been surprised. The others, perhaps, but not Dwight.

SIX

When we had come upon the Cheyennes, they hoped to kill a buffalo to relieve their hunger while on the march. Now with the fresh meat we provided, they were prepared to continue their move to the west.

The travois that had been drawn by a squaw was now hitched to one of our packhorses.

Davy Shanagan and the brave, whose name was Buffalo Dog, rode together, carrying on a conversation in sign talk with a word thrown in here or there. Listening to their conversation and to the other Indians, I soon picked up several words of the Cheyenne language.

One of the old men knew of a camping place, and keeping scouts out to warn of danger, we moved toward it. After a while, Shanagan joined me at the point. "They're ridin' to join their people," he said. "There's a plenty of Cheyennes up yonder. These Injuns figure to take after the Utes. Get their ponies back."

"Let's stay out of it. No use to make more enemies than we have."

"Now that may not be just that easy," Shanagan said. "They'll be wanting our help."

The Cheyennes preferred a camp on the open prairie but not too far from woods. The old man's choice was a good one, and just before sundown Cusbe Ebitt killed a buffalo cow. We gave most of the meat to the Indians.

Shanagan explained that the Cheyennes were convinced by my clothing that I was a great chief. "Let 'em think it," he added. "It makes us big men in their eyes. Prestige . . . that's the key word with Injuns."

We made our camp closer to the woods than the Cheyennes, but within a hundred yards of them. Firewood was plentiful and the stand of trees offered some shelter from the increasing wind. Moreover we liked the background of trees against which our bodies merged and blended. Our fire we placed in a hollow behind the stump of a broken-off tree where it was perfectly masked.

After collecting sufficient fuel for the night to come and the preparation of supper and breakfast, I moved to the point of the woods overlooking the plains. The position provided an excellent view in all directions, and sitting down just inside the belt of trees, I gave some thought to the situation.

The government of the Spanish colonies was a jealous one, permitting no trade with anyone but the Indians, and guarding against trespass. Captain Fernandez, as a diligent soldier, would have orders to resist any encroachment upon what was believed to be Spanish territory. From him, we could expect nothing but trouble.

Since I'd joined the mountain men, no plan of action had been discussed. We were riding toward the western mountains for a season of trapping and exploration. If all went as we hoped, we would find a favorable location and build winter quarters before snow fell, and if our trapping was successful, we could expect to return to Saint Louis in the spring with a bundle of furs.

Riding in company with the Cheyennes, who by virtue of our contribution of meat accepted us as part of their group, we could avoid trouble with at least one tribe of Indians. If a large party of Cheyennes were waiting ahead of us, we might easily have been ambushed because any unattached party was fair game, but now that we had joined this group, we would be accepted.

Faint sounds from the camps behind me only served to emphasize the stillness of the plain before me. The sun was gone but light remained, and a sky shot with crimson arrows from beyond the horizon. Shadows gathered in the hollows among the low hills . . . a wind stirred the grass, then the trees . . . there had been a lull, a moment of stillness. In the east there was a mutter of thunder . . . still far off.

For the first time, I found myself wondering what I had done. Behind me lay the career I might have had, a career as a teacher, an author . . . perhaps even in politics, for my friends were well situated in all these areas.

Few men had better educations, few had read so widely in so many fields, and now I had left it all behind. With the sudden death of my wife and son, my life had begun to seem empty and pointless. I had come west on impulse, and what lay behind it I did not know. Was it a secret desire to die? Had I come west for that?

Or to lose myself in a land far from all I knew, from old memories and old associations?

Rising, I walked back to the fire. Talley was squatted beside the coals roasting a chunk of beef, and the smell was good. Kemble was cleaning his weapon, giving it all the care a mother would give a child.

Ebitt came up to the fire, carrying some knots and large fragments broken from a stump. "Are you from Boston, Scholar?"

"From Virginia, and then Carolina. When the war ended, we moved near Boston. We lived in the country not too far out."

We talked campfire talk while the coffee came to a boil and the meat roasted. Meanwhile we ate wild onions dug from the prairie soil.

"My family worked with iron," Ebitt said. "I had no taste for it then, but one day I'll go back." He looked up at me. "We did ornamental ironwork. Pa considered himself an artist."

"Some of them were," I said. "I have seen the screen in the cathedral at Nancy, done by Jean Lamour, and the staircase in the town hall . . . beautiful work. And there was always Malagoli of Modena."

Ebitt lowered his chunk of meat, looking up at me. "Were your people in iron, too? I've heard my father talk of such men. They were the masters!"

"You're a smith, then?" I asked him.

He lifted his hands to me. They were square, powerful hands. "Iron is in the blood. Once a man has worked with it, it never leaves him. Yes, I was a smith, but I grew restless thinking of the western lands. At nights I would lie in my bed and think of all that vast, open land . . . unridden and untouched. One day I shouldered a pack and started out."

"There's no telling about wandering men," Talley commented. "They come from everywhere. I knew James Mackay. He was west in 1784, and again in '86, '87, and '88."

Kemble agreed. "Truteau was an educated man. Jean Baptiste Truteau. He came from Montreal, taught school for a while in Saint Louis, I hear . . . that was about '74, but some years later he was in the Mandan villages, trading. He lived with the Arikara, too."

We made our plans. Of the lands toward which we were moving we knew nothing but hearsay. There were furs . . . we did know that, and once in the mountains we had no doubt of our ability to find them.

For three days then we moved steadily toward the setting sun. We rode the flanks or point along with Buffalo Dog, and we saw no enemies. Several times we killed buffalo, and once an antelope. The Cheyennes were well supplied with meat, and the wounded brave grew better. Soon he could walk a little, and on the day we reached the hollow near the North Platte, he was able to ride. His name was Walks-By-Night, and he had counted many coups.

He rode beside me. "Why do you give us meat?" he demanded.

"You need meat," I said.

He was not satisfied, but after a while he asked, "Where do you go?"

"To trap fur in the western mountains," I said. "First, I must have horses. This," I said, "is a splendid animal, but he needs

time to learn to feed upon your grasses. He will learn, but in
the meantime he should not be ridden as hard as I must ride. I
shall need a western horse."

"I will give you a horse," Walks-By-Night replied. "When
we come to our people, I have many horses."

"It would be a great gift. I have nothing to give Walks-By-
Night."

"You have given meat to my people. You have ridden beside
us when the Utes might have come, or the Pawnees."

To that I made no reply. Our presence might have contributed to their safety, and it was well that he believed so, for we
wanted their friendship.

"You do not count coup? You take no scalps?"

How to explain that without offending him or seeming weak?
"The Great Spirit knows of my victories. It is enough."

"Your medicine is strong," he said.

Yet we rode with care. The air was cooler, the wind a little
stronger, and the coulees deeper. The greater the distance
from the settlements, the greater the danger. We were all
aware of this, and aware, too, that we were being watched.
Twice tracks were seen where horsemen had observed us for
some time, and by now they knew our numbers. Without
doubt they also knew of an encampment of Cheyennes to the
west, toward which we were obviously pointing.

If they wished to destroy us, they must attack soon, and
Walks-By-Night was aware of this, as was Buffalo Dog.

We found a camp in a shallow place where there was green
grass from a seep, and a few gooseberry bushes growing about.
One lone ash tree grew nearby and there was a dead tree lying
on the ground.

While the others made a fire, Walks-By-Night and I rode a
circle wide about the camp, scouting every rise in the ground,
but we saw nothing but a few buffalo.

During the passing days, my meager supply of Cheyenne
words had increased so that with it and what English Walks-
By-Night knew, we managed to communicate. I was also acquiring some skill with sign language, and then to my surprise I
discovered that the Indian talked very passable French.

He shrugged at my astonishment. "Many French trapper,"

he said. "All the time they come. Live in village. Ride with us. My people long time lived beside Great Lakes, then beside river far to north."

"This is not your homeland then?"

"No. My people lived north of Great Lakes in what you call Canada. The Cree were our people, too . . . far, far ago. All Indians have moved. No Indian lives where he once lived."

"It is the same with us . . . with all peoples. A long time ago our ancestors lived in what we call Russia . . . or beyond in Central Asia. Then they came west . . . many, many people came west, and some of them occupied empty lands, some took lands by driving others out."

"They were white men?"

"Yes. There was not one migration, but many. The horse made it easy for them to move, and with the horse to ride they became more powerful."

"It was so with us," Walks-By-Night said. "The Sioux have become strong with the horses."

We dismounted on a hillside. There in the sand around an anthill he drew me a rough picture of the western Great Lakes and showed me where once his people had lived and how they had moved west to the Cheyenne River in what was now the lands of the Dakotas or Sioux.

The Sioux had got the horse by trade or by theft from southern Indians who had them by theft from the Spanish. And once mounted the Sioux had pushed west from their homeland to conquer much of the Dakota lands of Nebraska, part of Montana and Wyoming.

It was growing darker. "Some say you people came from here"—I sketched in the northern steppes of Siberia—"and that you migrated across this water to America. They say my people came from here too."

He put his finger on the western Tarim and southwestern Russia. "And you from here? Then once our people may have ridden together . . . there?" He put a finger making a wide sweep of Central Asia.

"It could be," I said. Standing up I gathered my reins and stepped into the saddle. "Your people went east and north, mine went west and south, and now we meet again . . . here."

"It is far? This land we come from?"

"Very far. Perhaps three hundred suns of riding . . . perhaps more."

"We have come far." He looked at me. "We have come far to fight again here."

I smiled. "But not you and me, Walks-By-Night. I think there is friendship between us." I held out my right hand. "Between us let there never be blood."

"Only of our enemies," he said.

So we rode into camp together, and dismounted by our fire.

"See anything?" Kemble asked.

"A few buffalo . . . nothing more." I cut myself a chunk of meat and began to roast it over the fire. Walks-By-Night had gone down to his own people.

The meat smelled good, and I was hungry. I thrust a stick into the coals and a few sparks went up . . . disappeared.

I began to eat my meat and listen to the campfire talk.

SEVEN

We were noticeably higher when we moved out in the morning, the air was cooler, and the vegetation was changing to shorter grass, drought-resisting plants. Yet it was the Cheyennes that interested me most of all, and whenever possible I led Buffalo Dog or Walks-By-Night to talk of their people.

The horse had revolutionized the Cheyenne way of life, and once the horse had arrived in numbers, the Indians had almost ceased from planting, and had become meat eaters, buffalo hunters. Their way of life was in many ways easier as well as more dramatic. The Cheyenne lived upon the herds much as did the wolf, but the wolf could only kill the poorer stock while the Indian looked for fatter, healthier animals. The white man, when he came in numbers, would do the same.

Yet much of their killing was wasteful, for often the Indians would stampede a herd over a cliff, killing great numbers, although much of the meat would inevitably rot. Such a way of life could support only a limited number of Indians, but constant warfare and occasional blood feuds kept down their ranks.

In the distance we could see a faint line along the horizon and gradually I began to realize it was a far-off mountain range.

Excitement grew within me. Soon we would be there and settled down to the business of trapping.

Suddenly Shanagan came racing to me. "Scholar! *Look!*"

Atop a low line of hills to the south, several warriors had appeared. They sat their horses, watching us.

Sliding my rifle from its sheath, I made ready for an attack. But Buffalo Dog went racing by us and out upon the plain, calling out to the strange warriors. Slowly, they began to ride down off the ridge and we saw there were but four.

Walks-By-Night was beside me. "They come. Our people."

The four, riding a wide open line, rifles at the ready, came down the slope to meet Buffalo Dog. They drew together, stopped, and there was much talk. Meanwhile we had halted the column.

Now they came toward us—four warriors, one of them scarcely able to sit his saddle.

We had the story before the sun was high. They had come up to the Ute encampment, found it empty. Warily they had approached up a draw. Two lodges stood there, a fire was burning, nobody was in sight.

A rifle lay across a bundle of furs; a pot was over the fire; there were saddles and equipment lying about. The horses were tethered among the trees back of the lodges. Emerging from the draw, the Cheyennes were sure they had come upon a camp where the Utes were gone buffalo hunting.

They went into the camp. One Cheyenne stooped to lift the rifle; another started for the lodge nearest him. Suddenly there was a burst of fire. Three Cheyennes dropped where they stood, the others scattered, running. Another fell as he ran.

Hidden in their lodges, with holes made in the buffalo hide tepees from which they could fire, the Utes had waited until the Cheyennes were in their camp and at point-blank range.

The Cheyennes had recovered some of their horses, most of which had been lost in the chase that followed.

Was Fernandez with them? He was.

"Likely it was his idea," Sandy commented. "That's one we owe him."

"The Utes need no ideas," Talley replied. "I never knew an Indian yet who needed help figuring an ambush. They dread

an ambush more than anything, and use it themselves when
they can."

"I'm for cuttin' loose," Bob Sandy said. "Let's clear off from
these Cheyennes and head for the mountains. They move slow,
and it'll be dead cold before we make it."

"You're forgetting those Cheyennes up ahead. If we leave
these people, they won't know we're friendly."

"I don't know that I am," Sandy replied coolly. "An Injun is
an Injun. If we leave this lot, they'll kill us first time they see
their chance."

"I don't believe that, Bob," I said. "If we were strangers to
them, it might be true, but now we know them. We have
ridden with them."

"You think like you want, Scholar. Them books will teach
you plenty but they'll surely not help you savvy Injun ways.
You got to learn them firsthand."

"I appreciate that, Bob, but I still believe this party of
Cheyennes are our friends."

Sandy shrugged. "Maybe. But I notice you don't leave that
Ferguson rifle lyin' around. You're in more trouble than the rest
of us, Scholar. There ain't an Injun in America who wouldn't
give ever' horse he owns for that rifle. It ain't only the way it
shoots, but all that silver foofaraw you got on the stock. To an
Injun that's prime."

No doubt what he said was true. Certainly the weapon I
carried was a beautiful specimen of the gunmaker's art, and
such a weapon was rarely seen on the western plains, although
occasionally some trapper or Indian would decorate his gun
with brass studs. Sometimes this was a design, more often his
name or initials in the rifle stock.

Few of the Indians had seen my weapon fired, almost none
of them at close range, and so far as I knew, none of them
realized the rapidity with which it could be loaded and fired.
Yet I knew enough of Indians not to underrate them.

There had been a time in the eastern areas when a group of
Indians approached a number of white soldiers and asked them
if they would not extinguish the matches with which they fired
their guns. They protested that the sight of the flaming matches
frightened their women and children. Obligingly, the soldiers

did so, and then the Indians promptly attacked and killed all but one man, who fled into the woods and escaped.

The Indians had been shrewd enough to see that the musket of the white man had to be fired by a lighted match, although supposedly the Indian knew little of such weapons. The Indian was endlessly curious, quick to observe and to comprehend, and quite able to make minor repairs on damaged weapons. To underrate either their intelligence or their skill would be dangerous.

Over our campfires and when riding, we discussed the question from all aspects. We did wish to be about the business of trapping, but there was even more to be gained by trading. Alone of all our party, I possessed no trade goods, so whatever I had would be from trapping alone.

The hunting jacket and leggings begun back along the trail had been completed, and I now wore them, packing my other clothing away for state occasions.

The country grew increasingly rough. The ridges were often topped by thick brush or trees.

There were thousands of antelope, and twice we saw herds of wild horses that fled at our approach. Once we came down to a muddy spot, almost an acre in extent, trampled by wild horses. There were wolves about. We counted two dozen in the last hour of our march, and once we were in camp they lurked nearby.

During the night, I was awakened by something tugging at my pillow and sprang up to find myself facing a large wolf. Our bacon was wrapped in burlap, several sides of it together, and then placed in canvas bags for ease in packing. I usually used one of these bags as a pillow, and it was this the wolf had smelled.

Rifle in hand, I glared at him and he glared right back, growling. He stood over the bacon and seemed of no mind to give it up. On the other hand, bacon was a delicacy out here and all too little remained. Nevertheless I disliked firing at the animal in camp, and knew it would immediately awaken everyone who would spring to arms, believing an attack was in progress.

Tentatively I took a step nearer, looking into the wolf's

yellowish eyes, gleaming in the firelight. He snarled more fiercely, bristling and ready to fight, but when I took a step nearer he hesitated, then when I stepped quickly forward, rifle poised, he broke and fled. Gathering up the torn sack, I brought it back into camp.

Glancing at my watch, I saw the hour was thirty minutes past three. The sky was clouded over and I could see no stars. The wind was picking up and the air was cold. I added some sticks to the fire, which blazed up pleasantly, so I tugged on my boots and filled a cup of coffee.

Sleep had left me, and I was as wide awake as if it were morning. The wind worried me for no small sounds could be heard through its rustling and movement. Degory Kemble was on guard and I moved away from the fire to where he watched from some small brush.

"It's a wild night," he whispered, when I was near. "I've had a notion something's moving yonder, but I'd not want to wager upon it. Sometimes I'm sure I've heard something, and then it seems to be nothing. I'm glad you're here. Now both of us can be fooled."

We were silent, straining our ears against the wind for sound, and then we heard it, a momentary sound through an interval in the rising wind.

A shot . . . and then another, but far off . . . lost upon the wind.

"It wasn't that, but something nearer by."

"Who would be shooting? Not many Indians have guns. Captain Fernandez, perhaps?"

"At what? That sound was afar off . . . a half mile or even a mile."

We waited, listening, but we heard nothing more. Suddenly our horses snorted, stamping and tugging at their picket rope. Getting up, I went quickly among them, quieting them, but listening as I moved.

Something was out there . . . but *what*?

We did not awaken the others, waiting for what would develop. The horses were wary, apprehensive of something, yet they did not act as they would if there were wolves. As the horses quieted, I left them, listening into the wind to catch the slightest sound.

From the camp of the Cheyennes, there was no sound. I could see the faint, reddish glow of their fire, but nothing more.

So we waited out the night. Toward morning I dozed near the fire, awakening only to stir it up for cooking our breakfast meat.

Ebitt picked up the canvas pack, hefted it, then looked inside. He glanced at me. "Did your wolves come back? A slab of bacon's gone."

Degory Kemble glanced at me, then walked over and slowly inspected the ground. Our own feet had trod so much upon the grass that no other tracks could be seen.

"It was no wolf," Cusbe said, showing us the rawhide strings. They had been untied, the bacon taken.

"It's them thievin' redskins," Bob Sandy said. "Give 'em a chance an' they'll take the camp away, and everything that's in it."

"Is anything else missing?"

Talley checked, as we all did. A small sack of meal was gone, and perhaps a half pound of powder that had been left in a sack.

"Odd," Talley muttered. "There was a full sack alongside, and my bullet molds and some lead. That wasn't touched."

We exchanged a look, and then Solomon Talley shrugged. "A thief who takes only the small things," he said, "and not much of that."

"But a thief good enough to Injun into our camp whilst it was watched," Davy Shanagan said. "I've a thought it was the Little People."

Cusbe Ebitt snorted. "There's an Irishman for you! Something he can't explain and it had to be banshees or the like! I'd say we should move out."

We saddled up, and saddling Kemble told of the distant shots we'd heard, and of something moving in the night. Nobody had any comment, but when I rode out to take the point, Buffalo Dog was with me, and he had heard the shots.

The land was vastly broken now, with jagged upthrusts of

rock here and there, a difficult land to guard against, for at every step there were places where an enemy might hide, and a man must ride always ready, and no dozing in the saddle or depending upon the other fellow.

We were a hundred yards ahead of the others, entering a gap between low, grassy hills, when Buffalo Dog pointed with his rifle.

For a moment I did not see it, then I did. Blood upon the grass, blood still wet.

Isaac Heath was closest of them and he came riding to see what it was. He looked at it. "You heard shots, all right, and whoever was hit was hard hit. That's a sight of blood."

Buffalo Dog was looking up the slope, studying the brush and rocks at the top. Leaving Heath to point the column, the Cheyenne and I went up the slope, our rifles carried ready for a quick shot if need be, yet even as I rode I was agreeing with Heath. Whoever had lost that much blood was not going far.

Nor was he.

We found him among the first rocks. He was a slender man, well made, wearing buckskin leggings but a uniform coat, badly torn now and stained with blood.

We looked slowly around, but he was alone, and no horse was with him, nor any tracks of a horse. Kneeling, I turned him over, and he was dead, his sightless eyes turned wide to the sky.

He was a white man, and he clutched a worn skinning knife . . . nothing else.

Buffalo Dog scouted about, but I looked at the man. Here was a strange thing, a mystery, if you like. Who was he? How had he come here? At whom had he been shooting? Or who had shot *him*?

The man's features were well cut . . . he looked the aristrocrat, yet when I saw his hands, I could not believe that. The nails were broken, the fingers scarred, the hands calloused from hard work.

Davy Shanagan came up the slope. "Ah, the poor man! But where did he come from, then? There's no chance he was alone."

"There was at least one other," Talley said dryly. "The man who shot him."

"Aye," Cusbe agreed. "That's a bullet wound. And in the night." He glanced over at me. "And no Indian, or he'd have lost his hair. There's something a bit strange in all of this."

"Captain Fernandez," I suggested, "was farther north than he should have been. Farther north than he had a right to be. Could he have been chasing this man?"

"That's a Spanish uniform," Talley agreed. "He may be a deserter."

Carefully, I turned back the coat. There were pockets on the inside, and in the right side pocket there was flint and steel and a stub of pencil. There was blood on the pencil, blood on the edge of the pocket. I glanced at the outflung right hand, and there was blood on it, too.

The column of our people had halted in the gap below, and Solomon Talley turned toward them. "We'd best move on," he said. "This is no place to be come upon by Indians."

He went off, moving swiftly, and Cusbe followed. Shanagan moved after them. "Leave him," he said. "What difference does it make whether it's wolves or ants? It'll be one or the other."

Buffalo Dog was prowling about. I opened the man's shirt, feeling something beneath it. A gold medal, hung from a gold chain. A fine thing it was, of fine workmanship, and not the thing any casual man would have.

I took it from him, and then noticed the ring with its crest, and took that. In a small pouch under his belt there was a square of paper with a crudely drawn map upon it, three gold coins, and two small silver buttons each bearing a Maltese Cross. I didn't recognize any landmark on the map.

I pocketed the pouch after placing the ring and the medal within it. If there was any way of discovering who the man was, these small clues might help.

Buffalo Dog rode back to me, and dragging the man's body into a crevice in the rocks, I piled brush over it. There was no time for anything else. Yet the puzzle would not leave me.

In the saddle, I indicated the man's body. "Could you trail the killer?" I suggested.

He shrugged and we rode back to the others. The last of the Indians was just coming through the gap and Walks-By-Night was with them.

Buffalo Dog went off toward the head of the column and I began scouting around, cutting for sign, as they say.

Walks-By-Night joined me, and I told him what we had found.

"Who killed him?" I wondered. "And why?"

EIGHT

W alks-By-Night let his eyes scan the slope of the grassy hill. "He walks there, I think, where the grass is bent."

He had better eyes than I, for at the distance no bent grass was visible to me, but riding closer we found a trail. And there were drops of blood upon the grass.

It was then I told him of the missing bacon, meal, and powder. He listened, saying nothing, obviously puzzled by a thief with opportunity who took but one slab of bacon, and only powder but no lead.

"Either we have a thief who took only what was desperately needed or one who did not wish to carry more than that."

"It was not this man," Walks-By-Night said.

A thought occurred to me. "The shots had to come a few minutes before four o'clock, and something was bothering our horses about that time. Whatever or whoever stole our bacon and meal evidently was outside of camp when the shots were fired."

He stared off into the distance, and after a moment held up two fingers, then made the sign for together.

The bacon thief and the dead man together? "If they had

been together," I suggested, "they must have had a camp last night."

Warily, we backtracked the wounded man. He had fallen several times, but each time had struggled to his feet.

His back trail led us to a saddle in the low hills where we approached with some care. The Cheyenne motioned me to wait and hold the horses while he crept up to the crest of the nearest hill.

After a moment, he motioned me forward. Coming down from the hill, he slipped to the back of his horse and we crossed the saddle into a shallow, grassy valley. At the head of the valley, not two hundred yards off was a small clump of cottonwood and willow, and the greener grass of a seep or spring.

Two antelope were near the spring. They moved off as we drew near, evidence enough that no one else was close by.

Yet among the trees we found the remains of a fire, a faint tendril of smoke rising, and when we stirred the coals, a tiny gleam of red still existed.

Carefully, I looked about. Day by day my small skills in the wilderness were returning, and I was gathering more by watching and listening.

Walks-By-Night held up three fingers, and swiftly made the signs for man, woman, and boy.

"A woman? *Here?*"

It was incredible. He showed me the print of a riding boot, too small to belong to anyone but a woman.

There had been four horses, but the horses were gone, and there were no packs. We knew the whereabouts of the man, but what of the others?

Five men had come here searching. Walks-By-Night studied the ground with care, and then as we rode away, he explained. Much of it I had seen myself, but I could not read sign with his infinite skill.

"Five men come in the night . . . they find nothing."

"Then there's a woman and a boy out here alone? We must find them, my friend."

"You know her?" He was puzzled by my anxiety. "She is of your people?"

"She is a woman alone, with a boy. She will need help."

He asked many questions, and I tried to explain. No, I did not want the woman as a woman. I did not know her tribe.

Obviously the idea was foreign to him, for to most Indians any stranger was a potential enemy, and chivalry, by our standards, was alien to their thinking. Yet the Indian had his own chivalry, and that was the way in which I explained.

"It is like counting coup," I said. "To strike a living armed enemy is to count coup. To take a scalp is to count coup. According to the code of chivalry, to help the helpless is to count coup."

He was immediately interested, but he was growing restless. There were enemies about, both Indian and white, and our companions were drawing farther and farther away. We took time for a quick swing around to see if we could pick up the trail, and we could not.

As for the five men who had come to the camp, without doubt they were those who had killed the man whose body we found, but whom they had not found. Why?

The question was a good one. The trail had been easy to follow, the body lying at the end of it, but there had been no tracks to indicate discovery, nor had the body been searched except by me.

Had they been so sure he was dead? Or didn't they care? Then why shoot him at all?

Obviously they wanted something he had, yet nothing had been taken from him. Hence it was something he had that he did not carry on his person . . . or somebody.

Perhaps it was not he whom they wanted, but those he accompanied?

That would explain why once he had been shot and put out of the game they had not followed. They had followed the others.

Yet someone had slipped into our camp, stolen bacon, meal, and a little powder and escaped . . . not a girl, surely. But a lad now, a healthy, ambitious lad? There was a likely thing.

We rode swiftly to overtake the others, but the problem nagged at my attention. If the lad had come to rob our camp, and the now dead man had gone off in another direction, where was the woman? Or girl or whatever she was?

And what were they doing out here in the wilderness, and why were they pursued?

We rode down into the bed of the North Fork. There was much sand, little wood except driftwood, most of it half buried in sand, although growing on the bluffs in the distance appeared a few low trees that I took to be cedar.

When we came up to our party, they were encamped in a little valley where a fresh spring sent a small stream meandering down through a meadow. Near the spring there was a scattered grove of pines and cedars, gooseberries and currants growing in great profusion. We camped near them, their thorny wall offering protection from intruders on two sides.

There was wood, fresh water, and grass for our animals. All heads turned as we rode in. As I was stripping the gear from my horse, I explained what I had found and what we suspected.

Solomon Talley squatted on his heels, chewing on a long stem of grass. "Peculiar," he said, "mighty peculiar."

"I don't like to think of no woman out yonder alone," Ebitt commented. "Still, it ain't our affair."

"I've decided it's mine," I replied. "Do you go on and set up winter quarters. I'll follow when I've discovered what's happening here."

"You'll be killed," Kemble warned. "A man alone has a small chance."

"Somewhat more than a woman," I said. "Still, if one of us is to be a damned fool, let it be me. I'm better fitted to play Don Quixote than the rest of you."

"Don *who*?" Sandy demanded.

"Don Quixote," Heath explained, "was a Spanish knight who mistook a windmill for a giant."

Bob Sandy stared at him. "Why, that's crazy! How could a—!" He looked from one to the other of us, sure we were making a joke of him.

"There ain't no such thing as a giant," he scoffed. "Those are tales for children."

"I don't know," Kemble replied. "If you've never seen either

a windmill or a giant, one is as easy to believe in as the other."
He glanced at me. "If you want company, I'll ride along."

"Thanks," I said, "but this is a concern of mine. Do you ride
on to winter quarters. If I find a woman out there, she'll be in
need of shelter, and the lad as well."

"Are you sure they're together?"

I shrugged. "I think it unlikely there'd be several people out
here alone. I think for some reason the man we found dead, a
woman, and a lad started out upon the prairie. I think their
reason was drastic indeed, to attempt to cross the prairies
alone, and I think the five men pursuing them plan to recap-
ture or kill the boy and the woman as they killed the man."

"You reckon that was what the Spanish captain was after?"
Shanagan looked up at me. "His eyes were all over the place,
lookin' at everything we had, like he expected more."

To tell the truth, I wished to go alone and I think they
understood. Companionship is often to be desired, and to go
alone into the mountains or the wilderness is seldom a wise
course. Only a little help is sometimes needed to escape from
some difficulty, but on this occasion I wished to be alone.

For one thing, a man alone does not *depend*. When a respon-
sibility is shared, it grows less, and two men alert are rarely as
alert as one man who knows he cannot depend on anyone but
himself. It is all too easy to tell oneself, If I do not see it, he
will, and so a little alertness is lost.

"Davy," I told Shanagan, "I think we're watched. Once the
caravan marches, keep them changing places for a while. I'd
prefer they don't get an accurate count and realize I'm not
among you."

"I'll do it." He looked at me doubtfully. "You're takin' a long
chance, Scholar."

He was right, of course, yet the more I considered the
situation the more I decided I was right. The lot of us, if we
turned from our route, would immediately excite curiosity
from those who sought the woman and the boy, and if two
dropped out, that would not be missed, yet one would arouse
doubt that they had seen correctly. Moreover, I liked being
alone, and was sure that I could find them . . . or what was
just as likely . . . they would find me, if alone.

Some distance from our camp there was a rugged sandstone ridge, broken and shattered like a massive, uneven wall, with fragments fallen out from it and mingled with outcroppings. There was some cedar scattered among these ruins, and it was there, under cover of night, I took shelter with my horse.

With me I carried a good supply of dried meat, and so lay quietly. As the sun arose and our party prepared to move out, I lay motionless in the shadows of the rocks and watched and waited. Finally, they took the trail. Gnawing on a piece of jerky, I watched them trail away and disappear, and still I lay quiet.

When the strangers appeared, it was suddenly and without warning. They topped a low ridge and rode down to our camp, looking all about, examining tracks. Altogether they spent the better part of a half hour, just looking about. None of them were men who had ridden into our camp with Captain Fernandez.

During the night I had done a good deal of thinking. Our previous day's journey had been but twelve miles, very short for travel on horseback, but we had taken time in backtrailing the dead man and otherwise.

Now squatting in the shadow of the sandstone ridge, I drew a circle in the sand that was in my mind twelve miles in diameter. At the previous camp, food had been stolen from us by a lad, and a few miles into the circle a man had been killed, on that same night. Near one edge of that circle we had found their camp, and near the western edge was our own camp of the night. Somewhere in that circle or very close to it would be a woman and a boy, perhaps together again, perhaps waiting or searching. And somewhere here also were five desperate men, who also looked for them.

Seated where I was, I considered the terrain before me. The wounded man, I felt sure, had been attempting to draw the pursuers away from their quarry.

If the two were wise, they would remain where they were, wherever that was, because to find tracks someone must leave tracks, and if they remained still, their pursuers must eventually decide they had moved out of the area. Yet I doubted if two escaping people would have the patience.

Tightening the girth on my saddle, I mounted and rode down off the ridge, returning toward where the dead man's body had been left.

I was well armed. Aside from the Ferguson rifle, I carried two pistols in scabbards on my saddle, and my fighting knife, an admirable weapon in which I was thoroughly schooled.

NINE

The air was clear and cool. The thin grass of the country about was broken at intervals with outcroppings of limestone or sandstone, and there were occasional pines and cedars. Now, suddenly, the land about me looked strange.

Passing through a country is vastly different than searching it, and a land that had seemed simple indeed to me as a passerby was now complex, and filled with possible hiding places. I became increasingly both amazed and irritated with myself that I could have been so stupid as to believe the land unrelieved.

Now I realized that a thousand Indians might have been hidden where I would not have dreamed a dozen could find concealment. Secret folds of the land revealed themselves, and where there had been a long grass hill, suddenly I found that the crest of one hill merged at a distance with the crest of the hill beyond and in between lay a valley where a fair-sized town could have been hidden.

At first I found no tracks except the occasional ones of antelope and buffalo. Then twice I came upon the tracks of the grizzly, easily recognized from those of the other bears by the

64

long claws on the forepaws. The five riders had been scouting here also, and twice I crossed their trail.

The morning drew on, and methodically I searched every draw, every hollow, every clump of trees, and found nothing. Nor did I see any tracks that might have been left by Indian ponies.

If the lad had acted as I supposed, he had returned to some previously appointed meeting place with the woman. By now they had eaten, and probably were aware they were searched for by the five mysterious riders. Whatever hiding they had chosen must have been done on the spur of the moment.

From various vantage points I studied all the land about. One place seemed too obvious, another offered too little, yet more and more my attention returned to an outcropping of rocks on the southwest facing slope of a long hill.

From that point, our camp on the night we were robbed would have been visible. The lad would not have gone out on the mere chance of finding something at night in this remote region. He must have seen our camp and made his plans before dark. The route of the wounded man who had died near our trail trended away from that spot.

Allowing my horse to graze for a few minutes concealed by a clump of cedar, I studied the outcropping. It might be larger than it appeared from here; it also might offer a place of concealment.

A trail of greener brush and grass led down from the rocks into a widening fold in the hill. Apparently there was a spring or something of the kind there that subirrigated the fold and flowed down to what appeared to be a small, willow-bordered stream below.

The boy, at least, was canny. It had been no small feat to slip into that camp of wary frontiersmen and escape with loot. Small the boy might be, but he must also be something of a woodsman to achieve what he had without being seen or heard.

Determined to examine the place, I now gave attention to all the surrounding area. Where were the five mysterious pursuers?

The coolness of the dawn held on, and the wind stirred the sage, moaning among the cedars with a hint of storm. The sky was clouding over, and I was glad there was a slicker behind my saddle. Did the woman and boy have anything of the kind?

Warily, I looked around, my rifle easy in my hands, for this was a land of trouble and I was new upon this grass. These brown-turning hills did not know me yet, nor I them, and there was a menace in their silence, their emptiness.

At the touch of my heel, my horse walked down the long slope, angling across it toward the east. If watchers there were where the rocks crouched upon their hillside, they must see me now.

Suddenly, I felt good. I could trust myself, and I had something meaningful to do. My horse began to gallop and I found myself singing "The Campbells Are Coming!"

Down the long hillside to the thin trail below, down over the grass to the waiting ascent. I should climb the slope to—

They came out of a notch of the hills riding toward me, five hard-faced men with rifles in their hands, who drew up as they saw me coming. I did likewise, my heart thumping but my Ferguson balanced easily in my right hand, my fingers closed around the action.

Two wore Mexican sombreros although they were not Mexicans, one wore a coonskin cap, the others nondescript felts. Four wore dirty buckskins, one a frock coat. They drew up facing me.

"Good morning, gentlemen!" My voice was cheerful. "A fine morning for a ride, isn't it?"

"Who might you be?" The speaker wore the frock coat. He was a broad-faced man with a black beard and a disagreeable air to him, a burly man who looked likely to have his own way in most cases. I decided I did not like him.

I smiled. "I might be almost anybody," I said flippantly, "but as a matter of fact, I'm Ronan Chantry, professor of law and literature, student of history, lecturer whenever he's invited. And who might you be?"

They stared at me. I knew that if I disliked them, the feeling was mutual. I also realized they possessed an advantage: they would have no hesitation at shooting me if so inclined.

It was an advantage they had for the moment only, for as

soon as I reached that conclusion, I decided I would have no compunctions at shooting them either, one or all.

Wild country and wilder circumstances can thus render all theoretical ethics a little less than a topic for conversation.

"It don't make no dif'rence who we are," the man replied roughly. "I want to know just what you're doin' here."

My reply was as rough as his. "It makes just as much difference who you are as who I am, and what I'm doing here is obvious. I'm riding. I'm also, if you wish, minding my own damned business!"

The man was shocked. He had been so sure he held the strongest position that my reply shook him. He stared at me, unable to make me out, and then I saw his eyes go beyond me, looking for my supporters.

"Look here!" he said roughly. "I want to know—!"

I cut him short. "Whatever you want to know, you've a damned impertinent way of asking. Now I have no business with you. If you have any with me, state it and be damned quick. I want to get on with my riding."

One of the men started forward angrily and my rifle twitched only an instant. "Hold it right there!" I said. "I have no idea who you are or what you want, and to be perfectly frank, I don't give a damn. Now if you want trouble, start the music and I'll sing you a tune. If you don't, get the hell out of my way. I'm coming through!"

They did not believe it. That one man alone would talk so to *them*. Obviously they fancied themselves of some importance and they could not accept it.

I slapped the spurs to my horse and leaped him among them. As I did so, I kicked back with my right spur raking the horse nearest me on that side. Instantly he began to pitch, turning the small group into turmoil.

My horse swung to my bidding and I held my aimed rifle on the head of the leader. "All right, *gentlemen!*" I said. "Do you ride or do I shoot?"

Oh, they did not like it! They did not like it at all! But they rode. Glumly, bitterly, they quieted their mounts and they turned their backs on me. One of them growled, "We'll be meetin' again, mister. This here ain't over."

"I sincerely hope not," I replied. "You're a surly, impolite, and dirty-necked crowd, and somebody should teach you some manners."

They rode off and I watched them go until the shoulder of the hill concealed them, and then I wheeled my horse and ran him down the trail for a good half mile at a dead run, not wanting to open a shooting war with five men out on the shortgrass plains. When I could, I turned up the slope and worked around behind the hill where the outcropping was. I had an idea whoever was up there, if it was not all imagination, had witnessed the recent meeting, and would be wondering about it.

Now I had need of care. The way before me was plain enough, but I wanted neither to be shot by those I wished to help, nor by those searching for them, so I took my way along the reverse slope, angling along toward the crest, hoping to top the ridge somewhere back and to the north of the rocks.

Several times I drew up to look carefully around. My own position was exposed, but the bulk of the hill lay between myself and my enemies. No one else was within sight. Nearing the crest, I dismounted, and rifle in hand walked slowly forward.

There was the sort of place I sought right before me. It was a slight break in the crest where erosion had cut out the sandy earth from around the rocks and brush, leaving a gap. I went to it. Trailing the reins of my horse, I crept forward on my belly and looked across the ridge.

The outcropping looked like a cluster of small stone buildings from here, with broken rock all about, and some brush as well as cedars. Beyond, I could see nothing. If watcher there was upon those hills yonder, he was well hidden, as I was.

As for the outcropping, if it was not now the refuge of those I sought, it certainly had been, for crossing the ridge right below me and angling toward the rocks was a dim trail, the sort that might have been left by one horse.

The afternoon was well advanced and there was no time for delay. Nor as far as I could see was there reason for it. Leading my horse, I crossed over the slope and walked into the circle of rocks.

They stood side by side, facing me, a rather tall young woman of perhaps nineteen or twenty, and a lad of about thirteen. They stood together, their backs against the flat side of a great square block of sandstone. She had auburn hair and hazel eyes and was dressed in what had been a handsome riding outfit of a style much in fashion when I was last in Europe. The boy wore buckskins and a sombrero. He had black hair and black eyes and he carried a rifle much too long for him.

"How do you do?" I said. "I'm Ronan Chantry, and if I can be of assistance, I'd be pleased."

"I'm Lucinda Falvey, and this is my friend, Jorge Ulibarri. He's helping me to reach the Mandan settlements."

"The *Mandans!*" I exclaimed. "But . . . but the Mandans are far and away to the north! Hundreds of miles!"

"That's true," she replied quietly, "but that's where I must go. My family have friends in French Canada. If I can reach them, I believe I can arrange to return to my home in Ireland."

Frankly, I was disturbed. I had not imagined anything of this sort, and had no particular desire to go riding off to the country of the Mandans. Not that I did not know something about them, for I did, indeed. They were a tribe of Indians who lived in well-built mud lodges in the land of the Dakotas, on the Missouri River.

"We had best get you out of here," I suggested, "before those men come back. They were pursuing you, weren't they?"

"They were . . . and are. They followed us from Santa Fe, but so far we've given them the slip."

She volunteered no further information and I asked for none. She was a lady in distress and I was, I hoped, a gentleman. And she was, obviously, a lady. Moreover, it was equally obvious she was Irish, as was my own family . . . not to say that my line was innocent of other blood. My noted ancestor, Tatton Chantry, the first of the name to visit these shores, had set us all an example by wedding a most lovely lady whose family was of Peru. She was the descendant of a Spanish grandee who married an Inca princess.

"I have friends farther along the way," I said. "We'll catch them, and then it'll be time enough to make plans."

She looked at me with great severity. "You have evidently misunderstood, Mr. Chantry. My plans are made. I go to the Mandan villages."

"Yes. Of course."

We mounted, and rode down the long hill toward the trail. They had two excellent riding horses, fine stock with more than a little of the Spanish Barb in them, and a packhorse as well. What the packs contained, I had no idea. But in view of the long journey before them, I hoped it was food. However, looking at the young lady, I would almost have wagered my last cent that it was clothing . . . and not the clothing of the trail either.

We rode swiftly. Their animals were in better shape than mine and were in any case better horses, so we made good time while watching the country for the five men.

Rather hesitantly, I inquired if she knew their identities or motives. She denied knowledge but somehow I only half believed her and warned her we were in danger.

"Oh, *them!*" She was scornful. "I saw it all. You sent them packing, and if they come upon us, you'll do so again. I have no doubt of it. They fairly trembled when you spoke to them!"

Well, now. That was not exactly the way of it, but how could I use what eloquence I possessed to prove to this lovely lady that I was less fearful than she imagined? They had gone, and I was nice enough to know it was simply because I had a momentary advantage. Had it actually come to a scrimmage, their leader would have been dead . . . but I would be dead also. It was an event that I did not contemplate with any enthusiasm.

She rode sidesaddle and she rode it with dash and beauty. She carried her head high, and if there was fear in the world, certainly she was unaware of it.

Yet there were questions that must be asked. "The man who rode with you? Who was he?"

She turned her eyes to me. "He was, as my father was, one of the Irish Brigade. It was he who brought me to my father in Mexico, and when my father was killed, he offered to help me escape."

"You must tell me about that," I suggested.

"All in good time," she replied quietly. She drew up suddenly, as did the lad and I.

Seven Indians sat their horses in the trail before us, seven Indians, armed and ready.

TEN

S uddenly, one of them pushed forward and it was Walks-By-Night. "We ride to meet our friend," he said.

"I am pleased that you have come. Had there been fighting, you could have shared the coups with me. I would be honored to fight beside the dog soldiers of the Cheyenne."

They were pleased, although they wanted not to show it. They formed around us as a guard of honor and together we rode toward camp.

Yet a far different camp it was. My friends and their Cheyenne companions had come up with the main body of the Cheyennes for whom they had been looking. The camp was a dozen times larger than before, and there were at least fifty warriors in camp, fine-looking men, all of them.

It was immediately apparent that Walks-By-Night was a considerable personage among them, not a chief, but a warrior, hunter, and orator of prestige.

The horse herd must have numbered several hundred head, tough little mountain ponies most of them. Many were excellent stock, and I found myself appraising them thoughtfully for my own horse was feeling the effects of hard riding on no other food than grass.

Lucinda Falvey kept close beside me and I did not find it distasteful. Brave as she was, these were the first wild Indians she had seen at firsthand and she was obviously nervous.

Davy Shanagan rode out to meet us as we came in, glancing at Lucinda with startled pleasure. "Howdy, ma'am!" he said. "If I were to guess, I'd say you were from the old land itself!"

"And you would be right, sir!" she replied pertly.

We rode to where the others were camped together not far back from a small stream. Degory Kemble looked from Lucinda to me. "Do you have the story yet?" he asked me. "How did a girl like that come to the western plains?"

"And why not? Is there something to be afraid of? If there is, I'm not!" she declared. "Where can an Irish girl not go?"

Beside the fire that night, roasting a small bit of meat over the flames—and a nice flush it brought to her cheeks—she told us her story.

Her father had been a colonel in the Spanish army, a man who had fled his own country as so many had. He was among those brave Irish lads who were called the "wild geese" and who left their island where there was hope of neither land nor advancement, to join the armies of Spain, Italy, France, and Austria. A good number of them had risen to rank, as General Alexander O'Reilly, in Spain, who had been commandant in New Orleans until sent for to return to lead the Spanish armies against Napoleon. He had died on the ship returning, and that had been an end to it, but one of Napoleon's own generals, Macmahon, was another of them, and the bold lad who gave his name to the finest Cognac, Hennessy, was another.

Colonel Patrick Flavey had come to New Orleans with O'Reilly and then had been sent to Mexico.

"What happened there?" Kemble asked.

"My father did well, for he was a brave man, and a leader of men, but he was sent north to put down a fierce tribe who killed a priest and burned a mission church. He did that, too, but in doing it, he saved the life of an old Indian who was being tortured by another officer.

"From this, some difficulties developed, just why I don't know, but the officer wasn't of my father's command and he made much of the fact that my father was Irish.

"The Mexicans loved my father, and not at all this other man, but he had powerful friends. They interceded and demanded the old Indian prisoner be taken from my father and given to the torturer.

"My father had no choice but to obey." The girl hesitated, quite evidently deciding to conceal something. "Almost immediately my father was ordered north. Several months passed, and suddenly I received a message from my father telling me to come to him, only to find when I arrived that it was not he who sent the message.

"He told me they had brought me to Santa Fe to use me against him. When I told him that could never be, he said that a man who must protect others was less strong than one alone, and they would get at him by threatening me.

"I suggested we escape, and he replied that he was considering just that. He went out that night and returned with Jorge and Lieutenant Conway. He would get horses, he said, and some maps from headquarters. When he returned, we would ride north for the Mandan villages, and then into Canada where we had friends.

"He left then, and Jorge went with him. We waited and waited, but when it was almost daylight, Jorge came running. My father had been killed and with his last words told us to flee . . . and we did."

We debated the question among ourselves. Whatever the cause of the trouble, this was no place for Lucinda Falvey, and it was up to us to get her to Canada where she might find friends.

"There's no use you leaving what you planned," I said. "I'll take her through to the Mandan villages at least, and farther if need be."

Ulibarri squatted near us. "It's a long way, and there are many Indians," he said, "but I promised the colonel that I would go, and I will." He looked around at me. "I was raised by Indians."

"Hopis?"

"Apaches," he said, "but I speak much Indio . . . many tongues. I know the Sioux and the Pawnee and Shoshoni. I am young, but I have traveled."

"I will ride with you," Davy said suddenly. "She's an Irish lady, and far from home, and I'm an Irishman."

"I'm not Irish," Kemble said, "but I'll ride along."

"There are furs in the north," Solomon Talley said, "as well as here. We can trap as we go. The Hudson Bay Company will buy our furs."

There was no dissenting voice among them, and so the decision was made. Yet that night as I lay staring up at the stars, I considered the question. Obviously it was not the girl alone they sought, but what she knew, or what they believed she knew.

What secret had they attempted to torture from the old Indian? A secret he had told Falvey? Had that secret been passed on to Lucinda? Or to Conway or Ulibarri?

I remembered the few odds and ends from Conway's pockets. Was there a clue among them? I decided I'd have another look at that map.

And when morning came, I thought, I'll have a long talk with Lucinda Falvey.

For her to escape was of course essential, but to be penniless upon the world would not be pleasant for a young and lovely girl. Yes, yes of course she was lovely. That her father was one of the wild geese was obvious, that he might have a family to whom she could return was possible, but not too many of the Irish estates were paying well these days. A bit of smuggling on the side always helped, of course. My own family had tried it, too. There were still some of my blood remaining in Ireland, although only on my mother's side. How well off they were, I did not know.

I could think of nothing that would so arouse feelings as gold, and no doubt somewhere in this affair there was treasure involved. Of course, there was no shortage of treasure tales, and according to marketplace gossip, dozens of mule trains had gone north out of Mexico with treasure belonging to the Aztecs. Some of this was reported to have been hidden in western America, although why anyone should go so far to hide it, I could not guess, for the mountains of Mexico were filled with good hiding places.

There was no need to go more than a day's march from the valley of Mexico to find a thousand places where treasure could be hidden, so why anyone would travel hundreds of miles, risking discovery all the way, was beyond me.

The Aztecs were reported to have come from somewhere in the north, and many were the stories of just where that had been, but they were not a rich people when they began their long trek to the south, nor for a long time after their arrival in the valley of Mexico. It was unlikely that coming into possession of great treasure they would send it all those many miles back to a land they had themselves abandoned. Yet this was a land where gold had been found, and who could guess what might not have been found . . . and hidden?

So if there was a treasure, and if we could find it now, there might be enough to give Lucinda Falvey the advantages such a girl should have.

The night wind stirred the leaves, down in the Indian encampment quiet had come at last, and my eyes closed. A few spattering drops of rain fell, and half-consciously I felt them, then turned in my sleep and awakened.

The camp was still. Nothing seemed to move. The coals were red, with no tendril of flame remaining. I was awake, and wide awake, listening to I knew not what.

Tonight we had posted no guard, trusting to our Indian friends and their dogs. Lucinda Falvey slept near me, and beyond her, the boy, Jorge Ulibarri. Davy Shanagan lay just beyond the boy, and Degory Kemble on the other side of me.

My hand closed on a pistol butt, and I waited. What had awakened me? Suddenly, I knew. For as if a ghost, I glimpsed the faint outline of a man standing on the very edge of our camp, just beyond Davy Shanagan, and he was looking at Lucinda.

He was a tall man, and I could see his face, which was extraordinarily pale, like the face of a dead man, yet his eyes were black, and he wore a black hat, the brim turned up leaving his features clear and sharp against the night.

He did not see me, for where I lay there was shadow, and if

he saw anything of me at all, it was merely a form half outlined in the darkness. He was looking at Lucinda, and he held a knife in his hand. He started to move, then hesitated. He must step past Shanagan as well as the boy, and he did not like it. The slightest wrong move or sound and those around her would awaken, and he would be caught.

He did not like the odds. I could see the hesitation, the debate in his mind. One of them and he might have chanced it, but two he dared not chance, and with both Kemble and myself close by as well.

The dogs had quieted. There was no sound but that brief spatter of rain. For a moment I was tempted to shoot, yet I did not know the stranger, and he might well be a friend, although not for a moment did I believe that.

Who was he?

He was no man I had ever seen before. Certainly he was not Fernandez or any of his men. He was a stranger, but that he was a man of evil I had no doubt. Nor had I any doubt that he wished to either kill or capture Lucinda.

Gently I eased back the edge of my buffalo robe and thrust out the muzzle of my pistol. Yet even as I did so the tall man turned slightly and I saw his other hand held a pistol. He lifted it and aimed it not at me, but at Lucinda. His eyes were boring into the darkness as if he could actually see me.

"You might kill me"—he spoke very softly—"but I would certainly kill her."

My pistol still covering him, I stood suddenly to my feet.

But he was gone. . . .

Swiftly I stepped over the others to the edge of the woods, and there was no one there, nor was there any sound. At that moment the rain began to fall harder and I stepped into the woods. There was no one there.

Davy Shanagan was sitting up. "What is it?"

"There was someone here," I said. "Keep an eye out."

A swift search of the small patch of woods brought me nothing. Wherever he had gone, he had done so swiftly and with no nonsense about it. Beyond the patch of woods, there was open prairie and there seemed no place where a man could hide.

Skirting the woods, I returned.

"Sure you weren't dreamin' then?" Davy asked.

"He was a tall man, very pale . . . with black eyes."

"Maybe it was a ghost you saw," Davy said. "What man could come up to this camp without arousing the dogs? And never a yelp from them, not a yelp. Not from the horses, either."

Had I been dreaming?

"It was no ghost," I declared, "and he spoke to me."

"I heard nothing," Davy said, "and I'm sure I would have."

Both of us lay down again, but I slept fitfully from then on, disturbed that any man could approach our camp so easily. When morning came, I scouted around but found no tracks, nor did Davy. I began to doubt my own senses, and when I opened the subject at breakfast with Lucinda, she shook her head.

Yet when I described the man, she turned very pale. "Why! Why, that's what my father looked like!"

"But your father's dead?"

"Of course, he is! At least I was told so, and I believe it. But if it were my father, he would have come into camp. He would have spoken to me."

"A ghost," Davy insisted, "you've seen a ghost, man."

"Bah!" Bob Sandy said roughly. "There's no such thing as ghosts. He had a dream . . . or a nightmare, if you like. I've had them myself, and often enough. But mine were mostly with Indians in them, and I had a many in the years after my family were killed by those screamin', howlin' redskins."

"After this," Talley said, "we'll post a guard, tired though we may be. I want no man, nor ghost either, for that matter, coming into our camp unknown to us."

Our plans had been made, and now we went among the Cheyennes to trade for extra dried meat, and to make our preparations for the north. We would ride north, skirting the eastern face of the mountains, and once past them we would turn east of the mountains toward the villages.

"We will be coming out on the open plains in the winter," Kemble said. "It's asking for trouble unless we've more luck than we deserve."

"I can take them alone," I said.

Isaac Heath turned on me. "Are you more gallant than we are? I think not, Scholar. We will go with you, for alone you would never make it through. No offense intended."

"I take none. I know it would be difficult."

"We'll trap on the way," Ebitt said. "We must have something for supplies for another season."

My eyes went from one to the other, knowing what this meant to the lot of them. This was their life. To me it might be my life, but also might be only an interlude. I was not dependent upon furs as they were. A little money remained in an eastern bank, and a profession whenever I wished to return . . . if I ever did.

"Thank you. I appreciate this, and so does Miss Falvey."

"I do!" she exclaimed. "Oh, I *do!*"

And so we prepared ourselves for the march to the north, and said nothing more of it.

Yet I remembered the tall man with the pale face. Of one thing I was sure. He had been no ghost.

ELEVEN

There was no immediate taking off. There was planning to do, and equipment to put together. I sat long with Walks-By-Night and talked of trails, of game, of mountains. He had often hunted far to the north, and had gone north on raids against the Crow.

Finally, I showed him the map. After some thought, he recognized the place and gave me clear directions. Of this, I said nothing.

Meanwhile Walks-By-Night presented me with a lean, powerful Appaloosa, a horse he swore to me was the finest buffalo horse he had known. My own horse went to Feather Man, who traded me a buckskin and a zebra dun for pack-horses.

Finally, we put our packs together. The Cheyennes had little food to spare, but they let us have what they could, and it was noble of them, with a long winter to come.

The morning was frosty but clear when we started out, a few stars still hanging in the sky. Solomon Talley led off, riding beside Degory Kemble, Sandy and Shanagan followed, and then the dozen packhorses, followed by Lucinda and I, with

Ulibarri riding herd on the packhorses. Cusbe Ebitt and Isaac Heath brought up the rear.

We rode out, down into the riverbed and along it at a good clip. We wanted distance between ourselves and the encampment, hoping our disappearance would not soon be known.

We no longer feared pursuit by Captain Fernandez—we were going north, clearly out of Spanish territory—unless he was after the girl. And we did not think it was he who had followed her from Santa Fe.

Leaves were falling from the trees that morning, yet many had only turned red and gold with autumn. We left our friendly stream bed and turned up another, strange to us, but one that flowed down from the north.

Lucinda was silent, reluctant to go, yet appreciating the fact that we had no choice but to move and swiftly. As we rode, she became increasingly disturbed and I noticed her eyes going to the sun as if trying to determine our direction.

"If you have anything to say, better say it now."

"What?" Her eyes were suspicious. "What do you mean by that?"

I shrugged. "It's obvious, isn't it? Someone follows you from the Spanish colonies. Why? Because he believes you have something he wants, or you can tell him where it is.

"The man I saw, the one you said resembled your father, he didn't look like a man who would follow a woman for love. He might take a horsewhip to one, but follow her . . . no. He looked like a man interested in only two things: money and power."

"I don't know him."

"He knows you, and he'll be following us."

"You don't think we've slipped away from him?"

"That man? There isn't a chance. He'd be like a wolf on the trail. To be rid of him, you must give him what he wants."

"I will not!"

I chuckled. "And neither will I. But we must be prepared to run, to fight, and to run again. These men"—I gestured at those with us—"they risk their lives as well as their season's trapping for you. You might at least tell us what we're fighting for."

She was stubborn, and would say no more. Yet I was doing some thinking myself, and realized of a sudden that I might have the answer right in my pocket. I might have the answer in the items taken from the pockets of Conway, before we covered his body. Startled, I reviewed them in my mind. Aside from the map, there were the coins—and the *buttons*!

We held to a good pace that first day, keeping in the bottom along the creek and under the trees. Twice we drew up to rest and each time one or more of us rode out to check our backtrail. We saw nothing, heard nothing.

"If I didn't know I'd be dreaming," Shanagan said, "I'd guess we've escaped them."

"Not the man I saw. He had the face of a cruel, relentless man, the kind who would never give up."

Here and there we found a few currants still clinging to the bushes, and we ate them eagerly, pleased with a different taste. Twice we saw grizzlies, one group of three, an old she bear and two cubs, were feeding on a hillside a good hundred yards away. She stood up to inspect us, watching carefully as we slowly rode by and continued on our way.

Twice we passed groups of buffalo skulls, all with the horns turned to the west, for the Indian believes this is good medicine for the future hunt. Yet we saw few tracks of horses, and no human tracks.

We were pointed toward the mountains, and we moved steadily, holding to low ground and avoiding exposure. Lucinda was quiet, devoting all her attention to the country. Several times she drew up to study some rocky projection or outcropping and she seemed increasingly disturbed.

When night came, we camped with the last light, dipping down off a bench into a grassy bottom where a swift-running stream found its way through a thick stand of aspen. The night was overcast with a hint of the rain that had been lingering all through the day.

Nobody seemed disposed to talk. All of us, I think, were gripped by the seriousness of what we had done. Despite the hour, Davy and Isaac set traps. The place was ideal for beaver, and although we had seen no dam and it was late to look for it, there were beaver runs all about where they had dragged young trees or limbs down to the water.

Over coffee I said to Lucinda, "If you have anything to tell us, it had better be soon, for we shall travel fast."

"Why do you say that?"

"Something's bothering you, and I believe I know what it is. You see, I was the first to find Conway."

"He was alive? He hadn't died when you found him?"

"He was quite dead. But there are formalities. One cannot just let a man die and be buried. There are people who must be notified. There would be someone inquiring about him, wanting to know what happened."

"There was no one. He was an orphan. He was a friend to my father and my father is dead."

"Perhaps. Nevertheless, I did not know that at the time."

"What does that mean?"

"I went through his pockets." Her breath caught and I thought her face went a little pale. "I took what there was for identification, or to pass them on to relatives."

"I've said he had no relatives. You can give them to me."

"Perhaps I shall. One of the items was a map. There were a few coins, and some buttons. Very unusual buttons."

"I know nothing about them."

For a moment I was silent. The others would be coming up to the fire soon. I fed sticks into the flames, and then said, "I do."

She was startled. "You *what?*"

"I recognized the buttons. You see, Miss Falvey, I'm a man of curious mind. I read. I also listen, and when interested, I inquire. When a man is dedicated to the search for knowledge, he may follow his quest down many strange paths.

"Having followed my curiosity as far as I have, it's not difficult to put a few things together. Your father was an interested man also, that much is obvious. By what means he first learned of this treasure we may never know, but that he knew of it as did Conway is obvious. The buttons are an indication."

"They were all there was left," Lucinda said. "When my father found the old church, the treasure was gone . . . already gone. He found a few buttons, the medallion . . . a few coins, and a gem the thieves had dropped in their hurry to be away."

"No doubt that's true, as far as it goes, but what about the old Indian? He told your father something. Told him enough, in fact."

She hesitated, her eyes searching mine. "I must have help. Can you trust these men?"

"They're risking their lives to help you."

"Or to find what I'm looking for?"

"Not too many men are to be trusted when gold is a matter of concern, or a pretty woman, but I believe these men can be trusted. I've found them men of principle, and despite what many wish to believe, there are honorable men in the world.

"However, think of this. If you go away now, without the treasure, how will you get back? There're a thousand stories of lost cities, lost temples, vast treasures. Why should anyone believe yours rather than any other? How many men will you find who'll go into Indian country with you?

"There's another thing. Suppose someone finds it while you're gone? We don't know if that old Indian was the only one who knew. That man who looks like your father . . . what does he know?"

What I said was true and she knew it. Her chance of ever returning to this area was slight, yet she hesitated, twisting her fingers and thinking.

I could well understand how she felt. She was a young woman alone, far into a situation she had never expected or planned for, and even if she escaped from this wilderness, she faced abject poverty in a world without mercy.

She found herself among strangers, with a group of rough-seeming men with no allegiance to anybody or anything. That I was Irish she knew, and Davy Shanagan, too, but there were rogues enough among the Irish so that might count for nothing.

"I don't know what to do," she said helplessly. "I . . . I have no one. When I came to Santa Fe, I didn't expect this. Mr. Conway was going to help, and Jorge. I trusted them."

"And now you must trust us."

She looked at me, her eyes imploring. She must risk all or lose all. "You . . . you knew about the treasure?"

"Yes. Such stories have always fascinated me, and this one
had some peculiar aspects that we needn't go into now. It's
actually two treasures, you know."

"I didn't know."

"It began in Malta. A renegade knight of Malta fled the
island with a gold medallion, some silver buttons cut from a
uniform, and a dozen precious gems. In Spain, fearing the
knights of Malta whom he well knew would pursue him, he
joined a force of Spanish soldiers who were going out to the
Indies.

"His idea was to buy a plantation on one of the islands and
settle down there. However, his pursuers arranged for him to
be arrested by the Inquisition. He was tipped off, and selling
one of the jewels, he smuggled himself aboard a caravel sailing
for Mexico. There he took service under an assumed name and
led several slave-capturing expeditions among the Indians. On
one of these, he came upon an abandoned church in a deserted
village. It was one of those ill-fated attempts that came to
nothing because of the fierceness of the Indians, and by the
time our man came upon it, the place was forgotten.

"At about that time, an Indian trying to curry favor offered to
tell him of a treasure if only the captain would release him from
the group of Indians he was returning to slavery.

"Our captain listened, and the Indian told him that when
Montezuma was taken by the Spanish, much gold had been
hidden to keep it from them, and he knew where this gold was.
He led our captain to it, the captain promptly killed him, then
with the gems he already had and the treasure just taken, he
made a cache in the ancient church and came away."

"I didn't know how it happened," she said. "How do you
know all this?"

"Most of it's a matter of record. Nothing is as secret as men
imagine. The Indian who tried to buy his way out had talked to
other Indians of what he hoped to do, and when their companion turned up missing, one of them told of it.

"One man likes the smell of gold as well as another, and
where there is honey, the bees gather. At headquarters they
had inquiries about a certain renegade knight of Malta, so the
captain was called in for questioning on both counts. Unhappily

for them, and for himself, he wasn't as tough a man as he imagined, and he didn't survive the questioning.

"All they succeeded in getting from him was that he knew nothing, had hidden nothing, and was being persecuted by the knights of Malta because he knew their secrets.

"The renegade died, but appended to the report on the case was information to the effect that he was believed to have hidden the gold in a church or mission chapel."

"I knew none of this!"

"It all happened long ago. I learned of it when I heard talk of it one night in France. Several of us were discussing lost treasures and vanished cities, the way people will.

"One of the young men was from Madrid, and he knew the whole story. Later, from curiosity, we investigated a little."

"But it was gone! My father learned somehow, or figured out, where the deserted church was, but the treasure was gone and even the few things he found were well hidden. Father believed the treasure had been taken out by night and the men taking it hadn't known they'd left anything."

"Probably. But the story doesn't end there. The two men who got it recruited a bunch of Indians and struck off to the north. That was very early . . . before Anza went to colonize New Mexico. The two men fled, and there far to the north one killed the other. Later he and several of his party were themselves killed by Indians."

"And then?"

"That's where you come in, if you know where the treasure is, and if it's still there."

The wind stirred the flames, and they whipped angrily. I added a few sticks, listening for the others. Out in the night a wolf howled . . . a wild, lonely sound in the darkness.

"It's been two hundred years!" she whispered.

"A long time. But out here, time has little meaning. Of course, it depends on where it's hidden. A riverbank now . . . that would be bad. Rivers change course, wash away their banks. Most other places it would be hard to find." I glanced at her. "He wasn't killed near here, you know. It was away over east of here, near a great settlement of Indians."

"I know. That's what they said."

"It wasn't true?"

"No. The story is that the two officers, Francisco de Leyva Bonilla and Antonio Gutierrez de Humana, started from Nuevo Vizcaya and went to a pueblo near San Ildefonso, or perhaps actually where that town now stands. Then they started east for the buffalo plains, intending to go north to the French settlements in Quebec. They had a fight and Humana stabbed Leyva to death. Humana was eventually killed at or near the Great Settlement, which was far out on the plains to the east, but he'd buried the treasure before the Indians took him east.

"They'd surrounded him, moved in on him, and although he wasn't actually a prisoner, he knew it amounted to that, so he buried what he had, intending to return for it. Of course, they killed him and he never returned."

"Do you know where the treasure is? We have a map, but it's not complete. Purposely so, I believe."

"We should reach the place any day now," she said evasively. But I thought she had answered my question . . . she knew!

We had talked long, and the others had been of no mind to disturb us. One of the men gathered leaves for a bed for Lucinda and she spread her blankets over them. I listened to the night, and I was not at ease. I remembered the face of the man I had seen . . . and it was not a good face.

TWELVE

Dawn broke slowly under a lowering sky, heavy with clouds. Huddled over our fire, we cooked our food, left it to pack our horses and saddle up, all of us sour-faced and wary. Trouble was upon us and our every instinct spoke of it.

The coffee tasted good, and under the warmth of it and the comfort of the blaze, our spirits rose. Solomon Talley suddenly got up. "Do you stay quiet," he said. "I want to look about."

Shanagan threw his dregs on the ground. "I'll ride along," he said.

I had told them we were getting close, and they were ready for it. Cusbe Ebitt, a silent man most of the time, stopped beside Lucinda. "Do you not worry, miss. We'll see you safely to the States or wherever you wish, and with whatever is yours." He glanced around. "I speak for all here."

"You do, indeed," Degory Kemble said.

"We ride into Indian country," Isaac Heath said, "and they'll be many, we'll be few. Bob, I'll hope you rest easy on the trigger and invite no trouble. I know how you feel about Indians."

"I'm no fool, Isaac. I'll invite nothing, but if some Indian

88

should cross my path on the way to the Happy Hunting Ground, I might give him an assist."

"We are all on the way," I commented gently. "A man is born beside the road to death. To die is not so much, it is inevitable. The journey is what matters, and what one does along the way. And it's not that he succeeds or fails, only that he has lived proudly, with honor and respect, then he can die proudly."

"It's no wonder we call him Scholar," Kemble said dryly.

Jorge Ulibarri had been standing beyond the fire, and now he spoke. "I think they wait for us."

Kemble looked around at him. "Ambush?"

"No. Not yet. I think they know a little where the gold is, but not enough. I think they hang back, waiting for us to find it, and when we do, they'll come to take it from us."

"He makes a lot of sense," Bob Sandy said. "Boy, when this is all over if you want to ride with me, you can."

"Thank you. I must see the senorita to safety. It is a trust." He glanced at the ground. "Not many men have trusted me. Senor Falvey did." He looked around at us, puzzled. "I do not know if I am a man of honor, but he considered me so, and in this case at least, I must be."

"Like I said," Bob Sandy said, "anytime you want to ride with me. The offer stands."

A brief spatter of rain fell. Wind whipped the leaves and the grass. "We're going to get wet. We might as well get wet movin' as settin'." Ebitt got to his feet, tearing at the last bit of buffalo meat on his stick.

We put out our fire, and left the last of the coals to the rain. I went to my horse and swept the saddle free of water with my palm. Then I put a foot in the stirrup and swung to the saddle.

The others mounted, but we lingered briefly, wanting Talley and Shanagan to be with us.

"They'll foller," Sandy said. "We'd best move."

The way led up a draw between low, grassy hills. Before us the land grew rough, off to our right lay a vast sweep of plains, rolling gently away to an horizon lost in cloud. Huge thunderheads bulked high, a tortured dark blue mass that seemed to stir and move, but flat beneath where lightning leaped earthward.

More spattering drops fell, but we rode along, feeling the hard smack of the big drops on our slickers, keeping our guns under cover, fearful of dampened powder. As we moved, all were aware of those who followed, and each in his own mind was assessing the risk to himself and the party.

The draw narrowed, the walls were now steep, tufted with brush and occasional cedars, but craggy with outcroppings of rock. A trickle of water ran down the draw past us, a widening trickle that increased. Heavy rain was falling somewhere ahead of us and the draw became a canyon that narrowed considerably.

Degory Kemble drew rein. "We'd best hunt ourselves a way out of this. If we get caught in a rush of water, we'd be swept away, drowned without a chance."

My horse walked forward. "I think I see something ahead," I suggested. "There . . . back of that boulder."

It appeared to be a trail of sorts, mounting the bank, then angling on toward the lip of the canyon.

"We'll be out in the open," Kemble said dubiously.

"Better in the open than drowned," Ebitt said grimly. "Let's try it."

The horse I had from Walks-By-Night was a good one, so I turned him at once to the bank. He started up, scrambled on the shelving surface, then dug in and got to a place where he could walk. Soon the footing was better, and in a few minutes I had topped out on the lip of the canyon.

The world I faced was wild and strange. Before me was a fairly flat area some hundred yards in width that stretched on ahead for some distance. On the left of it was a steeply rising mountainside covered with pines, and the area before me had scattered pines and a few cedars with a forest of huge, weirdly shaped boulders tumbled from the mountain in some bygone age. From under my hat brim, I studied the terrain as best I could.

Low clouds hung threateningly over the mountains, far down the sides and seeming only yards above my head. Thunder rumbled, and as the riders behind me scrambled up the bank, the rain came down in sheets. Starting my horse, I walked forward, my hand on my pistol butt, expecting anything.

Tufts of grayish cloud hung ghostlike into the space before

me; thunder rumbled again. No trail led where we rode and there was no evidence that any living creature had gone before us. We wove single file among the tumbled boulders, isolated trees, or clumps of brush or cedar. What tracks we made would not last long in this downpour, nor was the land over which we rode liable to leave good tracks even without the rain. Yet we had no doubt we would be followed. Without adequate reason, with only an instinctive sense of danger, we had come to realize that he who pursued us was something beyond ordinary, although we had no inkling of who he might be.

Was it Falvey himself? Was it not a man who resembled Lucinda's father, but the father? Had he somehow survived? But if so, why not make himself known to his daughter? Or was there some other thing here? Some hatred, some evil, some ugly thing of which we knew nothing? Did Lucinda know more than she told us?

I think these ideas were reaching all of us. I believe a certain doubt crept into our minds along with apprehension. An unknown enemy is always more of a threat than one known, and this was an enemy whose motives we did not know. Nor could we gauge his strength or his intent.

Bowed under the pounding rain, we moved steadily on, riding not one directly behind another, but a little scattered to leave less of a trail.

Davy Shanagan and Solomon Talley lingered behind, bringing up the rear at a distance of more than a mile. When they joined us at the nooning, they had seen nothing.

Our nooning was where a slide had thrown some logs and brush over a few rocks, making a partial shelter from the rain. Under part of it, we gathered our stock, and under the most solid corner, we ourselves. To anyone less exposed than we, it would not have appeared as shelter, for the great up-ended slabs of rock had simply caught the debris of a minor earthslide, including the trunks and branches of several trees. Yet it was shelter enough to hunch our shoulders against the few drops of rain and to put together a small fire where we made coffee.

One thing I had already learned was that exposure to the elements is a relative thing. The shelter a man demands who lives forever out-of-doors is considerably less than he who is used to four walls and a roof. And this I must say for Lucinda Falvey, she made no complaints, nor did she appear to be less comfortable than any one of us.

We talked less now, chatting a little of the commonplaces of travel, but not going beyond that. I will not say it was only apprehension that sat upon us, although it was there. Each knew we had entered upon a trail whose end must be trouble, serious trouble.

The nooning past, we wasted no time. Warmed by the coffee and still chewing on the jerky we had lunched upon, we moved out once again. This time it was Bob Sandy who fell back, acting as rear guard. The rest of us moved out, more swiftly for the first hour.

The scattered boulders had grown less, the trees thicker. We wove through the slender black columns of the pines, climbing higher as we went forward. Once for several miles we rode across a barren place of exposed sheets of rock, dark with rain, and in places running with a thin film of water. Then we dipped down into thicker forest where at times we rode in relative dryness.

Here we did find a trail, and not a game trail, but one evidently used by Indians. It was narrow, as theirs usually are, and followed the natural contour of the wooded hillside. It led, as naturally as could be, to an overhang where some ancient long-vanished stream had undercut the cliff. And there was shelter, blackened in one corner by many fires.

The light offered at least another hour of riding, but another such shelter as this was unlikely, so we drew up and swung down. There was some fuel partly protected by the overhang and we found more. Soon a small fire was going. Our horses were stripped and rubbed down, but Bob Sandy had not appeared.

Suddenly I went to my horse. "I'm going back," I said, and then changed my mind. "I'll go afoot," I said.

Kemble reached for his rifle.

"Stay here," I said. "If he's in trouble, one of us can handle it. It may be calculated to split us up."

Kemble hesitated. "Maybe you're right." He was reluctant

to remain behind, but one man can often do much, and I had the Ferguson rifle, which they had come to respect.

My rifle under my slicker to protect it from the rain, I walked out of the overhang and back down the path. Walking has ever been my favorite method of locomotion, and I walked rapidly, my ears attuned for any sound but that of the rain.

When a mile lay behind me, I began to walk slower, pausing occasionally to listen. Bob had been following at about a mile behind, and although he could have fallen back, I now felt sure that something was wrong. Before me, not a quarter of a mile away, I remembered we had crossed a clearing. Turning from the path, I went up through the woods, moving swiftly and soundlessly. The wetness of the forest helped, my moccasins helped as well, for I could feel any branch that might crack under my feet before I rested my weight upon it.

My new route took me higher up the side of the hill so the clearing lay below me. Suddenly, across the clearing at the edge of the trees, a good hundred yards away, I saw Bob Sandy's horse. Closer by thirty yards, and down behind a deadfall, was Bob himself. His rifle was in his hands and he was facing back the way we had come. Suddenly two men came out of the grass up there and started toward him. He swung his rifle to one, and there was no sound . . . missed fire!

Without thinking, my Ferguson came to my shoulder and I fired. One man stumbled, then fell.

Instantly, I reloaded. The other man had ducked behind a tree, mystified, I think, by the shot. It was likely they believed Bob dead or seriously injured, but now, after that shot, they believed his rifle empty, and the second man stepped from behind the tree and ran forward.

I took aim, held my breath, let it out easily, and squeezed off my shot. He had not seen where my first shot came from, and did not now. The bullet struck him, but not effectively, for he merely drew up in stride, then threw himself into hiding. I was already reloading.

Probably it was the unexpected shot that stopped the man more than the effect of the bullet, for I was sure it was a scratch at best. But now he was sure he faced two men rather than one. My rifle was loaded, and I moved up through the trees, hoping for a better shot.

And in that instant, I heard the faintest stir behind me. Turning swiftly, I dropped to one knee, and the suddenness of my move and the drop saved me. A gun roared, at close range, and a tree that was now behind me spat bark from a grazing shot.

I did not fire. My sudden drop had left me, through no intelligence of my own, in an excellent position. Coming down, I was sheltered by the broken-off stump of a lightning-struck tree. Over my head was the trunk of the tree itself, a portion of it still fastened to the stump.

Partial protection I had, and complete concealment. The unknown marksman had been too sure of me, silhouetted against the outer light as I was, but now I was hidden, and my drop had been so sudden he was not sure whether I had been hit or not. Above all, my rifle was in my hands, unfired. A pistol was a heavy weight behind my belt.

All was still. Listening for some sounds of reloading, the possible *clink* of a ramrod or some such slight noise, I heard nothing. Not far away, a shadow moved silently. I held my fire.

Someone was there. Despite the coolness, I felt the sweat break out on my brow. My mouth was dry.

Bob Sandy lay back there in the clearing, possibly in need of help, but the man in the woods wanted to kill me, and if I moved, he would do just that . . . if he had reloaded.

The advantage might be mine. A great drop fell from the tree trunk and ran a cold finger down my spine. It was growing darker.

"Move in from the other side, Joe." The voice was calm, having the inflection of an educated man. "We have him."

Nor did I move. I did not believe there was a Joe. At least, not here. It was a ruse, a trick, a device to make me move or speak. I did neither.

At my hand was a dead branch some eight feet long, and slender as a whip. Carefully I closed my left hand upon it, lifting it soundlessly. Now half the art of the ventriloquist is misdirection, so holding my own mouth close to the broken stump behind which I crouched, I moaned ever so gently and at the same time rustled the leaves several feet away with the tip of my branch.

He fired. I saw the blast of flame, heard the bullet strike, and I fired my Ferguson.

There was a sharp gasp, then a stumbling fall, but I waited no longer. Back I went through the trees, running swiftly and almost without sound on the soft earth and rain-wet grass and pine needles. I ran swiftly down the hill, circling toward Bob Sandy's horse.

As I neared the horse, I spoke. I had cared for him a time or two, and he knew me, pricking his ears and taking a step forward. In an instant, I was in the saddle and racing down into the clearing.

"Bob!" I yelled.

He came off the ground like an Indian as I charged up to him, bridle free, my rifle in one hand, the other down to help. He came into the saddle as if he had done the trick a hundred times and we left the clearing at a dead run.

Behind us, there was a shot. From the second man, I think. But that was all.

Slowing down, I said, "Are you hurt?"

"Through the leg. I've lost some blood, Scholar." As an afterthought he said, "Thanks, Scholar. I guess maybe I should read some of them books."

THIRTEEN

Once away and into the winding woodland trail, I slowed down. Bob Sandy was hanging on with one arm, the other holding his rifle. "You did some shootin', Scholar. How many did you get?"

"One," I said, "and either scared or nicked two more."

"The way you was shootin' they must have figured they'd tackled an army."

We rode up to the overhang and Talley reached up to help Bob Sandy down. "The Scholar saved my bacon," he said. "Had me dead to rights."

"We thought we heard shooting," Kemble commented.

While Cusbe Ebitt worked over the wound, I explained briefly, with comments from Sandy, what had taken place. Then Bob explained what began it. He had been riding along a good mile behind us, and suddenly they closed in and opened fire without warning. "I don't know what this outfit is after," Bob said finally, "but they mean business."

We gathered more fuel, cooked our meat, and sat about the fire. Several of us collected boughs for Lucinda's bed. Isaac and Degory built a crude shelter out in the woods and opposite the

cave where a sentry could watch in both comfort and concealment. We had scarcely finished these chores when we heard
the sound of a horse walking, and then a voice called out,
"Halloo, the camp!"

Hastily, I threw a corner of blanket over my Ferguson rifle.
There was no sense in letting them know what we had. Isaac
had stepped back into the shelter and sat quiet there.

"Come in with your hands free!" Talley said.

It was the leader of them, the tall, pale man I had seen in
the night. He wore buckskins but a planter's-style hat and he
rode a magnificent black horse.

He walked his horse into the light, and looked about, his
eyes missing nothing. At last they fell upon Lucinda.

"Well!" He bowed, removing his hat with a sweeping ges-
ture, the perfect cavalier. "My niece! It has taken me a long
time, my dear, but now we are together again, and thank God
for that!"

"I . . . I do not know you," she said, but her voice was
halting and frightened.

"Not know me? I am your father's brother, Colonel Rafen
Falvey, at your service. I've come to negotiate with these . . .
kidnappers for your release."

Degory Kemble said quietly, "You're misinformed, sir. Miss
Falvey is with us of her own choice. We're honored to be her
escort to the Ohio towns."

"Well, now, that puts a different look on the situation. I was
told my niece had been kidnapped, and rushed after you to
obtain her release." He dismounted, somewhat stiffly, I noticed,
like a man who might have been wounded slightly.

He walked up to the fire, and never have I seen a man so
cool, so completely in command of himself. Obviously he had
chosen to risk everything on a brazen demand for the girl, and
I admired the fellow's nerve. Yet when I looked at Lucinda, I
was worried.

This man who claimed to be her uncle was no more than
thirty-five, only a few years older than I, and he was handsome, debonair, and obviously educated. He carried himself
with style, and he seemed in no way disturbed that he was
among men with whom he had lately exchanged shots.

"Then, of course, there's no problem," he said cheerfully, extending his open hands to the fire. "Lucinda, if you'll get what you wish to take with you, we can be riding back to our camp. It's not far and we have a number of men, a much safer escort than this small group, if you don't mind."

For the first time, I spoke. "I'm afraid it's less simple than you seem to believe," I said quietly. "Miss Falvey is with us because she wishes to be. We feel ourselves perfectly adequate to escort her where she's going."

He looked at me. Some shadow of the overhang partly concealed my face so he was forced to peer. Yet my comment in no way disturbed him. "It's quite simple. It's better for a young lady of Miss Falvey's years to be with her family. I have nothing against you gentlemen, but of course, her own flesh and blood—"

"I don't know you," Lucinda said quietly. "I've heard my father speak of a half-brother of his who was a complete scoundrel."

Talley chuckled, and Rafen Falvey's face tightened. Yet a moment later, he smiled. "He was joking, of course. My brother and I often made such jokes. He always laughingly said I was the black sheep of the family, and he was the prodigal son who would sometime return.

"Come, Lucinda. Let's go. We've talked long enough."

She hesitated, and then she said, "I—"

Her reply was interrupted by Jorge Ulibarri. The boy had suddenly come into the light. Now he pointed his finger. "He murdered your father! He shot Mr. Conway!"

Rafen Falvey's face stiffened with anger. "You, is it? Next time you'll die."

Suddenly there was a pistol in his hand. "Lucinda, you'll come with me . . . now! And the first one who moves will die." He produced a second pistol. "And you, Lucinda, will be the next to die."

None of us had weapons in our hands. Nor were we within reach of any. My Ferguson was under the edge of the blanket, but I would have to take it out, reverse the muzzle, and then fire . . . much too late.

Isaac Heath spoke from the hidden shelter directly behind Falvey. "At thirty feet, with a rifle, Colonel Falvey, I'll not miss. My bullet will take away the base of your spine, and rip out the front of your belly. I don't think you want that to happen."

He was no gambler, I saw that at once. He was willing, even anxious to kill, but he did not want to die, nor to be left to die. With a rifle at his back, he had no chance and he knew it. I got to my feet and casually reached over to pick up one of my own pistols.

"I suggest, sir, that you ride out of camp. I further suggest that you keep riding. The next time I shoot I'll have a better target."

"It was you, then? In the woods back there? You're more of a woodsman than you look."

He was staring at me, a strange light in his eyes. "Ah? You very much resemble Ronan Chantry," he said. "In fact," he peered into my face, "you are Ronan Chantry."

"You have the advantage of me, sir."

"You fought a duel with a friend of mine. I was to have been his second but I was delayed and arrived too late."

"A friend of yours, was he? You should choose your friends with more care."

He smiled at me pleasantly enough. "I only regret his marksmanship. Had I been in his place, I would not have missed."

His arrogance angered me. "You had your chance this night, and you did no better."

If I have ever seen death in a man's glance, it was in his then. "On another occasion I'll do better. I'll kill you, my friend, and I'll enjoy it."

He turned his attention abruptly from me to Lucinda. "You'd do better to come with me," he said. "I at least might leave you enough for some gowns. That's more than you'll have from this rabble."

"They're gentlemen, sir. Can you say as much?"

He shrugged. "I care nothing for gentlemen or otherwise. I'll have you in a day or two, and whatever goes with you. When I'm through with you, the Indians can have what's left."

He turned sharply, looking from one to the other of us. "As for you, all that live will be staked to anthills, depend upon it."

Abruptly he mounted his horse, tucking one pistol behind his belt to do so, and without a backward glance, he rode off down the trail.

No one of us moved or spoke for several minutes, and then it was Solomon Talley. "We'd best not low rate the man. He's a scoundrel, no doubt of it, but he's also a damned brave man. It took nerve to ride in here and speak as he did."

I looked over at Lucinda. "He's your father's brother?"

"Half-brother, but an enemy to my father from childhood. I remember some word of him now, but I wasn't often with my father so I knew little of this man."

The rain had stopped and suddenly we had had our fill of the place. With only a few words to be assured that all agreed, we saddled up and started off down the trail, camped in an isolated clump of trees at nearly daybreak, slept three hours, and took to the road once more.

We had deliberately mentioned Ohio, hopeful that our pursuers would try a wrong direction, yet not very hopeful, at that. The Mandan villages were our destination, and it was a long ride and a hard one. First we must find the treasure, if treasure there was, and for that moment Rafen Falvey would be waiting.

Obviously he knew something, but not enough. He needed us to locate it for him, and we had no choice but to find it, and then take our chances on getting away.

I was worried, as I believe we all were. Rafen Falvey was no mean antagonist. To take him lightly would invite disaster.

Solomon Talley and I led off. "We must know more about him. How many men he has, how they're mounted and armed."

"That there's sensible. Trouble is we ain't got the time. Seems to me we got to keep movin', and when we get that gold we got to really light out."

The man to whom we had talked was not only intelligent, but shrewd, a knowing, conniving man and one filled with hatred. We must be on guard every second.

Talley and I discussed the question, and all the while, our

eyes and ears were alert for trouble. We believed we had a good lead on them, but to take such a thing for granted was to borrow trouble.

Twice we changed direction. Several times we descended into stream beds and backtrailed, emerging where a rock surface left little in the way of tracks, and then plunged into the deep woods. Deliberately we swung fallen trees across our path, chose unlikely ways, and all the while, we knew we might not be fooling them at all.

Bob Sandy rode right along. That his wound bothered him we knew, but he let us see none of it. "Only one thing to do," he said. "We got to lay in wait. We need to pick a good place an' cut them down as they come into range."

The thought had occurred to me, and I had no qualms about ambush. When facing superior numbers, any tactic is useful, and we knew they outnumbered us, and we also knew their leadership was uncommonly shrewd. However, if we waited in ambush, we would lose whatever distance we had gained, and might ourselves be surrounded and wiped out. We decided to move on.

Twice during the day I got out the map I had found in Conway's pocket, but could find nothing in the terrain that corresponded with what the map indicated. Unfortunately, we were moving fast, and I feared the map required a better overall view of the country. I began to get the impression it had been drawn from some vantage point higher than we now were.

There was, of course, the possibility we would find nothing. Two hundred years is a long time, and the Indian or those who told him might have told others. Treasure is ever elusive, a will-o'-the-wisp that has a way of not being where it is supposed to be.

Deliberately I chose a way that took us higher and higher upon the mountain, and when we camped that night, it was in a thick cluster of spruce trees with branches to the ground. To our right and rear there were aspens, a thick stand virtually impossible to penetrate without sound. Before us and beyond the stand of spruce, there was the mountainside falling steeply away and a green and lovely swell of meadow with occasional outcroppings.

"I'd no business getting you into this," I told them over the fire. "You'd have been trapping beaver by now had I not joined you."

"And I," Lucinda said.

"It's nothing." Degory Kemble waved a hand, dismissing our comments. "We're learning more of the country, and when we do begin trapping, we'll be the better for it."

Later, after the sun had gone down and when the land was light, I moved to the edge of the spruce and studied the country and the map.

No man can know a country seen only in daylight. The morning and evening hours are best, for then the shadows have gathered in the depressions, the hollows, and canyons, and the terrain is revealed in a completely different manner. Nor is the light at dawn the same as at sunset, although there are similarities.

Lucinda came out beside me, and we sat there, screened and shadowed by spruce, studying the terrain before us. After a moment, she indicated a shoulder of rock some ten miles off across country to the east and south. "That's a place I was to look for. We're very close."

"What is it we're to look for? How will we know?"

She waited several minutes to reply, and I could understand. Without doubt, it had been drilled into her to tell no one. That she had been told at all was simply the only kind of insurance her father could offer . . . in the event something happened to him, and to Conway.

Solomon Talley had come up beside her, but she hesitated no longer. "There's a great slope burned bare above a blue black cliff about twenty feet high. Above the burned area there's a slope of reddish yellow broken rock."

"Is that all?" I stared at her. I simply could not believe it, nor could Solomon. "Was there nothing more?"

"Across the creek bed there was a rocky face with a jagged white streak . . . like lightning . . . upon the face of the rock."

Neither of us said a thing. We just stared off across the

darkening hills, not knowing whether to laugh or simply throw up our hands. They were just such landmarks as a tenderfoot might choose . . . and utterly useless.

She looked from Solomon to me. "What's wrong?"

He poked at the ground with a stick, and I said, "Lucinda, in these mountains, and in any lot of mountains, you'll find a thousand such places. And as for that bare slope . . . there's hardly a chance that it's still bare."

"You mean . . . you mean it isn't any good? We can't find it?"

"I didn't say that. We do know it's near here. But you see, that Spanish officer expected to return. He knew the place. The landmarks he chose were no doubt taken quickly, with little time. He noticed the most obvious things.

"Such slopes are quite common high in the mountains, and as for the white streak, it was undoubtedly quartz and that's a familiar sight, too. It's evident this description originated from the Spanish officer. Any Indian with him would have observed differently."

She looked like she had been struck. Her face was pale. "Then we can't find it?"

"One chance in a thousand," Talley said, "but there must have been something else? Some other thing? A hint of some kind?"

"No."

We walked back to the fire and sat down. Talley explained briefly. We all felt sorry, not for ourselves, because we had lost nothing, but for her, who had lost everything.

We had come west after fur, at least most of us had. Why I had come I did not yet know. To run away from something? From everything? To change myself? Or to return to a lost boyhood?

"The joke's on him," Shanagan said, "that white-faced spalpeen from Mexico. After all, we did come after fur, and we can still get fur. He's got nothin' facin' him but a long ride back."

"But he doesn't know that," Ebitt replied gently. "He doesn't know, and he'd never believe it. He'd think we were lying. And you remember what he said . . . he'd kill us all . . . trying to make us tell what we don't know."

We looked at each other across the fire. The hope of treasure was gone; the long march to the Mandan villages remained. Nothing was solved.

And somewhere on our back trail, Rafen Falvey was riding.

FOURTEEN

We sat about our fire feeling very glum indeed, not for ourselves, for we had little to lose, but for Lucinda, for whom we'd all come to feel a great affection.

In a difficult and desperate situation, she had not complained. She had ridden with the best of us, she had calmly made do with what was available, she had said nothing about the food, nor had she asked any special privileges.

Suddenly angry, I looked over at Degory Kemble. "Damn it, Deg, we've got to do something! The stuff was hidden, and with information as poor as that, I doubt if anything has been found."

"How far from that promontory back there?" Talley asked.

"A day's ride," she said.

"And that might be anything from twelve to thirty miles, depending on their horses, their anxiety, and what they figured to do."

"It would be nearer the lesser figure," Cusbe Ebitt replied. "Think now . . . they had the treasure with them. Indians were already with them or closing in. We cannot be sure of just what the situation was after so long a time, yet they must have been pushed to let go of the treasure at all."

"Think of it now. They wanted to get away to the French colonies where they could return to Europe and live in style in Paris or London or Rome. They didn't *want* to bury that treasure.

"So they would have moved slowly, I think. They would have been looking for a place, something that offered a camp . . . a good reason for stopping . . . and something that offered some kind of a marker. Something more than we've been told."

"But I've told you all I know!" Lucinda protested.

Solomon Talley nodded his head. "I think you have. That doesn't mean there was nothing more. It's likely there was something they reserved for themselves, some knowledge they held back."

"My guess is that we're within five miles of it right now," Isaac said.

Firelight flickered against the dark spruces and the white trunks of the aspen. They were some of the largest aspen I had seen, for the aspen grows in thick stands, grows tall and straight. It is a tree that likes the sun, needs the sun, and it is one of the first to grow across burns where fire has swept. It grows up, grows tall, and then under its cover the spruce begins to grow, sheltered and protected by the aspen. Yet as the spruce grow taller, the aspen tend to die out, until after many years the aspen are gone and a thick stand of spruce remains.

One of the most beautiful trees anywhere, it is not a good timber tree, for it rots from the heart out. Now with winter coming on, the aspen had already turned to gold. The earth where we were to sleep was inches deep with the golden leaves . . . treasure enough for me.

Rising from the fire, I gathered leaves and heaped them into a place for Lucinda to lie, then bunched leaves for myself. I was restless and wakeful. Deliberately we had allowed our fire to burn down to coals. We fed it some knots and chunks lying about, but such as would smoulder and burn but would make no bright flame.

Bob Sandy's leg was bothering him. We had treated it as best we could, and though it was but a flesh wound, it was painful and his leg was stiff. He was first to sleep, then Ebitt.

Heath was standing the first watch, and was already on the

slope below us. Kemble and Talley both turned in, and then
Jorge Ulibarri, after finding there was nothing he could do for
Lucinda, went to sleep well back in the stand of aspen. Davy
Shanagan lay under a spruce, out of sight from but within sight
of the fire.

"Why do they call you Scholar?" she asked suddenly.

I shrugged. "It began as a joke, but I was a teacher briefly. A
restless one, I'll admit. Research I liked, teaching I liked also,
but I've done a bit of writing, and studied law somewhat. To be
frank, I've not fallen into a settled pattern. You see, as a boy I
lived much in the woods. The wilderness left its mark on me,
and I would find myself longing for the dark paths among the
trees again."

"And now what?" she asked.

"Who knows? I doubt if I'll ever go back to what I was. Of
course, there's much to be learned. I'm tempted to travel, to
explore more of the ancient civilizations in Asia. Or here, for
that matter. Too little is known about what happened here before
the white man came."

"You're not married?"

"My wife is dead. It was then I cast off my ties to all I'd
been." I got up. "You'd better rest. Tomorrow won't be easy."

She went to her bed, but I did not go to mine. There was no
sleep in me, and I knew not why. Something was disturbing
me, and in my restlessness I went to where Heath stood guard.

"You, is it? There's nothing . . . yet. But I don't like the feel
of the night."

"Nor I."

Our backs were to the stand of aspen. The leaves whispered
gently around us. The moon was rising, throwing all about into
stark relief. The white trunks of the trees were like Grecian
pillars. I put my hand on one.

"They're self-pruning," I said. "Their early branches fall
away when they grow tall."

"These are thick," Heath said. "Most aspen are more slender."

"These are a hundred years old or older," I said, "and they
rarely grow to two hundred . . . very rarely."

He turned his face toward me. "Chantry, I was thinking of
what you said earlier, that the aspen grows over old burns. And

it was a burn she spoke of. Do you suppose it could be covered by aspen?"

"I'll be damned. Heath, you're probably right. By now that slope would be covered by spruce, with few aspen left, if any."

"Or those left would be very old . . . like these."

We stood silent, thinking the same thought, that we might even now be standing among those trees, with the blue black cliff beneath us and the rock with the streak of quartz opposite.

"It's too much to expect," I said, "but Heath, do you keep watch. I'm going to see what the slope above us is like."

"Do that." He spat into the leaves. "I have a feeling about this place. Tonight when you talked of the aspen, I kept thinking of how it looked when we rode up here."

Turning, I skirted the aspen and went up through the gloomy avenues of the spruce. In the moonlight the aspen were beyond belief, the still white trunks, the gently wavering golden leaves . . . they possessed a magic of their own and it was no wonder so many animals and birds loved them.

I climbed steadily, working my way along, carrying the Ferguson rifle in my right hand. The climb was often so steep I had to pull myself from tree to tree, using handholds on the branches. Suddenly I was there, out in the open above the aspen, above the spruce, above everything. For this was timberline.

Turning, I looked around me. Up here I could see the moon. The sky was impossibly clear, bathing the forest below in misty golden light. Not the mist of cloud or dampness, but of moonlight among the trees. Behind me bulked the vastness of the mountain, below the steep hillside, the shimmering pool of the aspen, and beyond, on the far side of the valley bottom an escarpment . . . an ancient fault at the edge of the rugged tableland that lay beyond.

Of the valley itself I could see nothing. All was deep in shadow down there. For a moment I stood, lost in the impossible beauty of the scene, and then I turned to look at the steep slope behind me.

It rose sharply up to a rim against the sky, and as I moved to its foot, rocks crunched under my feet. It was what we had been looking for . . . a steep slope of rocks broken and shattered by changing heat and cold. A moment longer I waited and then, as I started downward, my ears caught a faint sound.

Quickly I turned and looked along the base of the talus slope. I could see someone walking toward me, a tall man. Instinctively I stepped back to more level ground and better footing.

He came on along, walking easily and almost without sound. There was no question in my mind as to who he was, yet I waited, curious what the man would do, and aware of our camp, just below.

"Greetings, my friend! I had a feeling only one man would be up here at night. It takes a man with a bit of the poet in him to come to such a place when he could be sleeping. Well, I'm glad you came. It's time we had a talk away from those others."

"They're my friends," I said, somewhat stiffly.

He waved that away. "Of course. We all have friends. What they mean to us depends on how we use them. I think yours have ceased to have value."

"My viewpoint is somewhat different."

"Ah? Of course. You'd be a romantic sort or you'd not have come west. And a bit of a damned fool, if you don't mind my saying so. You've nothing to gain out here.

"The sea . . . now that's another thing. When this is over, I'm going to get the handsomest ship on the water, and I'll round up some of my old crew and we'll show the rascals what piracy really is."

"If you ever hope to do that," I suggested calmly, "it would be wise to start now."

He laughed, turning his eyes to me. "Well now! Our Scholar threatens? Maybe there's something there, after all."

He gestured toward a flat rock. "Sit down, man. We need to talk. You and I . . . we have brains. That lot down there smells of the hides they take and of the life they live. They're nothing. Now you and me, that's something else. The world is ready for those strong enough to take it . . . and I don't want all of it, just freedom to do what I damned well please with a piece of it. All would be too much trouble."

He had seated himself on another rock. He leaned toward me. "I like you, Scholar. Let's go partners. If you want the girl

. . . take her. I don't want any one woman. Attachments are a bloody bad business. Take them and be rid of them, and off to another port in the morning.

"You and me . . . we could have that treasure between us. Oh, it's there! I know it's there! And not far from where we sit, either. What do you say? Throw in with me. You take the girl and one-third. I take one-third and we use the remaining third for expenses . . . for a ship.

"There's a schooner in New Orleans that can shake off anything on the water. We can take a couple of prizes, then off for the Indian Ocean. It's the best place, believe me.

"Can you navigate? You can? Fine! That will take some burden off my shoulders. I'm a dead-reckoning man myself, and there're times when it's not good enough."

He took a Cuban cheroot from his pocket and lighted it. "Look . . . I've twenty-odd men back there, and a tough lot they are. They can take that bunch of yours and chop them like mincemeat . . . but I happen to know there's a river that heads not far from here, deep enough to float a canoe. We'll leave the lot of them, take the loot, and float down to New Orleans.

"It's as simple as that. You know where the loot is. I have the canoe hidden. We can be two days gone before they realize and they'll waste themselves hunting for sign . . . the river leaves none."

I chuckled. "And the one man alive when the canoe reaches New Orleans has it all? Am I right?"

He laughed. "There! I knew you were my kind of man. No, none of that. You spoke of friends awhile back. A man may not need friends but he needs companions, and the devil of it is a man doesn't find many men who have brains, not many who appreciate the arts, music, books, ideas . . . a man needs somebody to talk to.

"No, we'll go all the way together. No throat cutting in the night, no double cross. And after we get to sea, we'll go halves on everything."

I got to my feet. "No, Mr. Falvey. I'll have nothing to do with it. My advice is for you to turn about and take your men

out of here. I doubt if there's a treasure, and if there is, we
don't know where it is. Nor does your niece.

"I'll admit we thought there was, but her directions turned
out to be flimsy, indeed. Why, there're fifty places within a
dozen miles of here that answer to her information! We leave
as soon as our wounded man is able to travel."

The smile had gone from his face. He shrugged. "Well, it
was worth a try. I half expected you'd be a damned fool." He
held out his hand to me, smiling. "No hard feelings?"

Instinctively, my hand went out. He gripped mine hard. "All
right, men, *take him!*"

I jerked hard on my hand, but Falvey had uncommon strength
and he hung on. Instantly, hearing boots grate on the rocks, I
threw myself into him. My move was unexpected and Falvey
staggered, fought for his balance, but when I threw my weight
downslope, he let go. I went flying, my left hand gripping my
rifle, and rolled and tumbled down the slope into the darkness.
Two shots rang out, then a third. At least one bullet clipped
leaves near me.

Falvey, who had fallen to his knees, was getting up, swearing.

I started to move, a branch cracked under my hand, and a
shot clipped an aspen trunk close to me and spat bark in my
face.

Yet I lunged to my feet and ran into the aspen, weaving in
and out among the trunks.

Another shot was fired, but there was small chance of hitting
me among the aspen. I ran on, heedless of sound, yet actually
making little on the damp leaves. On my left was a dark clump
of spruce . . . the camp should be there.

I plunged into the open, looking quickly around. Nothing!
Somehow I had lost my way among the trees, and—

But no.

The fire was there. The dark coals smoked slightly, and there
was a tinge of red where one still glowed.

Gone . . . they were gone.

I was alone.

FIFTEEN

Alone . . . they were gone. But where? And for how long?
My own gear was gone too. Everything had been taken but the fire. Were they captives? Or hearing the shooting, had they simply fled, imagining me dead, or if not dead, able to survive and find them.

Survive . . . that was the first thing, and to survive I must move.

An instant I held perfectly still, listening. Every sense put out its feeler, the wind, the stirring of brush. Carefully I eased back from the fire's faint glow, into the deeper shadow of the spruce. I could see nothing there, but neither could they.

Where to go? Higher there was no cover. Downhill toward water and easier travel was almost instinctive and therefore to be avoided. Along the mountain's face then, toward the north.

The spruce trees stood so close their boughs touched. Crouching I went under some, between others. My mind held the thought *like a ghost . . . move like a ghost . . .* and I did just that.

The thin moccasins sensed every branch, every thing under my feet. I felt my way swiftly along. Get away first, far away, survive first, and then find my friends and help them if they needed help. A dead Ronan Chantry was of no use to anyone but buzzards and coyotes. Along the face of the mountain. It was steep, but not too steep for travel. Here and there it was suddenly steeper, and glancing up, I could see the still peaks and shoulders of the mountain, majestic in the moonlight. I moved again, ran lightly for thirty yards, then paused.

The night was without sound. I waited, stilling my breathing, listening. Nothing.

Again I moved, more carefully now, angling slightly upslope. I wanted to see what lay above me in the open. If they were traveling there, they could pass me, move ahead, then cut downslope and I would be surrounded.

I saw nothing. Living in the wilderness had tuned my ears, made my senses more keen. I was more like the boy I had been than the student of later years. Now I was back, and in every fiber of my being I knew, this was my home, this was where I belonged.

Stopping suddenly I crouched close to the trunk of a spruce, under the drooping boughs. In the slight hollow there, I waited. Had I heard something? Or were my senses deceiving me?

A faint stir, and then a low whisper, only a few feet away . . . a dozen feet? Possibly less.

"He can't have come this far. He's a Boston man, not no woodsman!"

"Mebbe, but he surely done vanished into nothin' yonder, just when we had him."

"I tell you we've come too far. He's back yonder. If we let him get away, Rafe will kill us all. I tell you, that man *skeers* me!"

"So? You've et better, lived better, had more'n ever since you been with him. He scares other folks, too, and rightly. He'd kill you soon as look at you."

My knife was in my hand. If there was to be close work, I wanted to be ready for it, and there's nothing better for close work than a blade. Mine was two-edged, razor-sharp, and with a weighted haft . . . a beautiful fighting knife made a thousand years before, in India where they had the finest steel.

I had inherited that knife. Chantrys had owned it for a good spell. It had been given to an ancestor of mine by a Frenchman named Talon who got it privateering in the Indian Ocean, given to him by a girl. A pretty one, I would guess.

My rifle was in my left hand now, the knife in my right. I waited, stifling my breathing. I was even tempted to move out and attack them. I might get one before they realized anyone was near, but the other might shout and then they'd all be upon me.

My feelings at the moment were very unscholarly. I felt like a savage, as some of my Irish forebears must have felt at such a time.

The night was cool. Now my eyes could see their legs. Their bodies were obscured by the thick, low-hanging boughs.

"We'd better get on with it."

"What happened to the rest of them? That's what I'd like to know. They worry me. Solomon Talley was in that crowd."

"Talley? The hell you say! Then this'll be a tougher lot than Rafen thought. Talley wouldn't go to the mountains with a lot of tenderfeet."

They moved off, making only small sounds, and I waited, not wanting to lose all by too sudden a movement.

Evidently the others had escaped, or if captured, these two knew nothing of it. Well, where would they go? Down toward the creek I suspected.

Carefully, I eased from my dark shelter, and moving like a wraith along the pine-needled carpet beneath me, I worked my way upslope and along it. First, to escape. To get clear as the others had done. Then to find them.

A mile I covered. I was sure it was that, for I was skilled at judging distance. Then I found a place where rocks from off the rim had crashed into the trees, pushing some down, causing others to lean. The dark spruce boughs offered a shield and I crept into this place and sat down, suddenly desperately tired.

The tension that had kept me up was easing off, and the sleep I had missed was demanding repayment. Crawling back into my natural shelter, I carefully made sure I left no signs at the opening, and then with my knife gripped in one hand, my rifle beside me, I slept.

Daylight found an opening in the boughs and touched my

eyes. At once I was awake, but for a moment lay perfectly still, trying to remember where I was. The spot where I had taken shelter was one of those accidentally created places of which a number may always be found in the forest. Actually, it could have sheltered our whole party, exclusive of the horses, and the only trouble lay in the fact that while I could see a bit down slope, my view toward the crest of the mountain was completely blocked.

Sitting up, I looked down the slope but could see nothing, my view obstructed by the thick stand of spruce. I took up my Ferguson and carefully wiped it dry, slipped my knife into its scabbard, and moved to the opening.

There I waited, listening. Meanwhile, my mind searched for a solution to the situation. Lucinda knew, as did the others, that we were in the near vicinity of the treasure's location, so even if they had moved, I did not believe they would move far.

The difficulty lay in the fact that Rafen Falvey knew this also.

For the moment I was secure and it was a temptation to remain right where I was. After all, what did I owe to any of them? Why go out there and get killed or wounded and left to die when I was not involved?

Yet I was involved. Lucinda Falvey had put her trust in me and in my companions. I did owe them a debt, and surprisingly enough, I did not want to stay out of it.

It irritated me that Rafen Falvey should take me lightly, and there was something in the man that made me bristle. I did not think of myself as good, but I was quite sure he was evil.

On cat feet, I eased through my brief shelter of spruce boughs and looked about . . . nothing. Regretfully, I glanced down at my moccasins. I would have to repair or replace them, for this running over the hills was doing them no good, and moccasins had a short life in this kind of country.

Moving from tree to tree, I worked myself along and down the slope. Before me there was another, younger stand of aspen. When I moved toward the trees, I heard water running. The spruce scattered out, and in a slight hollow above where the aspen began I saw a trickle of water, not more than six or eight inches wide. Grass grew along it, and it seemed to have its beginning under the frost-shattered rocks above.

After a long look around, I lay down and drank my fill, then splashed the cold water on my face and in my eyes. Nor did I delay at the water, but stepped quickly over it and went swiftly down the hill to the edge of the aspen. From there I had a clean sweep on the talus slope that led to the crest of the mountain, and it was bare . . . empty of life.

No shooting . . . nothing.

Often as a child in the eastern woods I had played at Indian while hunting for meat, and now I moved much as I had then. Using the best cover, I moved along and down the slope, switching back suddenly to change direction, and then again. There was cover enough.

My view of the bottom was suddenly excellent. A long meadow through which the stream ran, aspens and willow at the stream's edge, a few cottonwoods, and some low brush I could not make out at the distance, and on the meadow a half dozen marmots were feeding.

It was a pleasure to watch them, for shy as they were, they would scuttle into their holes in the rocks at the slightest movement.

Seated perfectly still, I let my eyes range over the bottom where they were, trying to see any disturbance in the grass to indicate tracks. I found nothing. The trees along the creek were few and scattered, and except for an occasional cotton-wood, not large.

Where would my friends be likely to be? And where was Rafen Falvey?

Concentrating on these questions and studying the creek timber below and the scarp opposite, I scarcely noticed the piping whistle of the marmots. It touched my consciousness but made no impression until suddenly the lack of movement did. The marmots were gone!

Both hands gripped my rifle and I rolled into deeper cover and wound up lying prone, propped on my elbows, my rifle in position.

They came quickly, two men riding point, one of whom I'd seen before, and a dozen yards behind them, Rafen Falvey, then the others. It was as tough a lot of men as I'd seen. They rode on by, and then suddenly, Falvey shouted.

Instantly the two files faced in opposite directions and slipped the spurs to their horses, and each file charged into the trees. It was a move calculated to scare anybody in their path, and it worked.

One rider was charging directly toward me, and I shot him through the chest. He threw up his arms and fell, hitting the earth not twenty feet from me, dead before he reached the grass. For a wild, flashing instant I thought of grabbing his loose horse, but then I was running, charging into a thick stand of spruce, vaulting over a deadfall, and ducking among the rocks.

A passage like a hallway opened before me and I ran down it, then ducked right toward the mountainside. Behind me I could hear shots and yells and somebody was racing a horse opposite me, then on past. Behind the rocks and brush, I was unseen, but it would be a minute only until they closed in all around me.

A space too narrow for a horse opened on my right, and gasping for breath, I went into it, turned sidewise and edged through. A brush-choked hollow lay before me, but I thought I saw a place where animals had gone through, and dropping to my knees, I crawled in, and fortunately had the presence of mind to scatter some leaves behind me, and to pull down a branch so no opening was visible.

On elbows and knees, I wormed my way along the passage, if such it could be called. All around me was thick brush, much of it blackberry brush with thorns like needles. But wild animals had used this opening, and I made my way through.

At the end it opened on a sheet of bluish rock scattered with pebbles fallen off the mountain. There were slender aspens here, and I stood up and faced into them, loading the Ferguson as I went.

They were no more than a hundred yards away, and it would be only a matter of time until they found me. What I needed now was a place to hide. Or a place in which to make a stand.

Falvey was shouting angrily. Suddenly I heard a shot, then a burst of firing . . . and silence.

A moment I listened, but they would be searching for me, knowing me trapped against the face of the mountain. I went down the dry watercourse through the aspen, their leaves dancing overhead, and then turned and found myself with a sheer wall of rock on my right hand, a wall at least thirty feet high, and without a break!

The place was shadowed and still, dappled by sunlight falling through the leaves. I walked on, careful to make no sound. My enemies were close beyond the scattered boulders, brush, and trees on my left, and on my right a rock wall not even a squirrel could climb.

Soon they would discover it was not thick brush and boulders to the rock wall. They would find there was this ancient watercourse. . . . Suddenly it ended.

The rock bed along which I had been walking suddenly turned right, dipped slightly down, and came to an abrupt end.

From around that corner, back up the way, came a shout. They had discovered my hidden path. In a moment I would be fighting for my life.

Glancing quickly around I saw what I had not seen before, a black slit at the foot of the rock wall into which the water had evidently poured. It was narrow, but there was just a chance. Suppose it dropped off fifty or a hundred feet into blackness? I'd wind up in a cave with a broken leg and no way to get out. The thought was not pleasant.

Nevertheless, there might be a foothold, something to which I could cling—

Dropping to my knees, I lay flat, then backed my feet into the hole. Squirming back, only my shoulders, arms, head, and rifle still outside, I felt for a foothold.

And something grabbed me!

Before I could yell, I was jerked bodily back into the hole and tumbled in a heap on the sand at the foot of it.

There was a moment when I saw a grizzled old man in ragged, dirty buckskins, and then he was fitting a stone into the slit.

"Shush now!" he whispered. "They're a-comin' on the run."

I heard their boots pounding on the rock outside, shouts, then swearing as they found nothing.

We could hear them threshing in the bushes, hear boots

scraping on rock. "Hell," somebody said, "I'll bet he never came this way at all!"

The old man whispered. "We got to set awhile, let 'em work off their mad. They won't stay long."

I was too astonished to speak, and sat, clutching my rifle . . . only I wasn't. My hands should have been gripping my rifle and they were not. It was gone!

Faint light came from a crack around the rock that blocked my point of entry. The Ferguson rifle was in his hands, the muzzle pointed right at me!

SIXTEEN

The hands that gripped the Ferguson were gnarled and old, but they were also thick and powerful. "You jest set quiet, boy. I ain't about to let them find you. Or me," he added, with a faint chuckle.

Surprisingly, we could hear well. Their boots grated on the rock, they threshed in the brush, and then somebody spoke again, farther away, the voice coming faintly. "Nobody come this way. He's hidin' in the bresh somewheres."

Their footsteps receded, and I looked slowly around. The cave in which I sat was about twenty feet across, but longer, and growing narrower as it led away from the basin. Evidently the water had spilled through the crack, swirled around in here, then found its way out by a passage widened by years of erosion.

The floor of the cave was sandy with rock underneath. There was a little driftwood lying about, and on a shelf an old pack rat's nest.

The old man stood up. In his day he must have been a man of enormous strength. Even now his wrists were thick and strong. His shoulders were slightly stooped, like those of a gorilla. He turned from me and picked up his rifle, which he had leaned against a wall. At the same time he extended mine to me. "I was afeared you might be skeered an' take a shot at me, grabbin' you like I done."

"Thank you," I said. "You probably saved my life."

"Figured on it." He turned toward the passage. "Let's mosey out'n here. Ain't no place to talk, this here. When a sudden rain comes, this place fills up mighty rapid. Seen it a time or two."

He led the way into the passage. It was completely dark there and I had no liking for it, but he walked along fearlessly so I judged he not only knew the place well but also that there were no obstacles.

"Weren't always like this. I cleaned it up. Never know when a body might have to git out an git, an' when I take to runnin', I don't want nothin' in the way." After sixty counted steps, I saw light ahead, and then another twenty steps and we emerged in a much wider room where a little light filtered in from some crack above. Several openings left the cave.

"Seen you from above." He indicated with a lift of his head the mountain above us. "Seen them folks a-huntin' you. Seen you turn down the crick bed yonder, figured to help."

"Thanks again. That's a bad lot."

"I seen him before. Two, three years ago he came up here, poked around all over the country. I seen a Injun he got holt of. . . . That's a mighty mean man yonder."

His buckskins were worn and dirty, and his hands showed him to be old, but there was no age in his eyes.

"Are you a trapper?" I asked.

He chuckled. "Time to time. I'm a hunter, too, time to time. I'm whatever it needs to get what I want."

"My name is Ronan Chantry. I joined up with some others to trap the western mountains but we ran into a girl in trouble, and we've been helping her."

"Girl?" He snorted. "They're mostly in trouble, an' when they ain't, they're gettin' other folks into it." He loaded his pipe. "Who's with you?"

"Solomon Talley, Degory Kemble, Davy Shanagan—"

"Huh! I know Talley. Good man. An' that crazy Irishman . . . I know him, too. The others?"

"Bob Sandy, Cusbe Ebitt, Isaac Heath, and there's a Mexican lad with us named Ulibarri."

"I knowed some Ulibarris down Sonora way. Good folks. Sandy, he's that Injun hunter. I never cottoned to him much. I always get along with the Injuns. The Blackfeet . . . well, they're hard folks to get to like, although I expect a body could. The Sioux . . . they're huntin' me all the while.

"Take pleasure in it, I reckon, but they can't find me." His eyes glinted with humor. "Good folks, them Sioux! I wouldn't be without 'em. They come a-huntin' for my hair an' they keep me on my toes.

"Can't find me, nohow. This here mountain is limestone. Don't look it, because she's topped off with other rock, but this here"—he waved a hand about—"is limestone. This whole mountain is caves . . . must be hundreds of miles of them. I got me a hideout here with twenty-five or thirty entrances.

"I don't hunt trouble with no Injun, but when they hunt me, I give 'em a-plenty. Ever' time I kill a Sioux I post a stick alongside the body with another notch in it . . . nine, last count."

"And you?"

"They got lead into me oncet, arrers a couple of times, but I got more holes'n a passel o' prairie dogs, an' I always crawl into one of them an' get away. One time I ducked into a hole I didn't know an' it taken me three days to find my way to caves I knowed.

"Got 'em downright puzzled. They got no idea what to make of me. Last winter after an almighty awful blizzard I found the ol' chief's squaw, his daughter, an' her two young uns down an' nigh froze to death.

"Well, sir, I got a f'ar a-goin', built a wickiup, an' fetched 'em meat. I fed 'em broth and cared for them until the weather tapered off some. I fetched fuel an' meat to keep 'em alive, an' then when I spotted some Injuns comin', I cut a stick with nine notches, then a space, an' I added four crosses to stand for them I took care of. Then I taken to the hills."

"You're a strange man, my friend, but an interesting one. Mind telling me your name?"

"Van Runkle. Ripley Van Runkle. You jest set tight, now, an' in a while I'll show you a way out of here. Your folks are holed up yonder. You say you got womenfolk along?"

"A girl . . . Lucinda Falvey."

"Kin to Rafen?"

"She's his niece, but he's a thoroughly bad one, and trying to get what rightly belongs to her."

"Hmm, now what might that be?" His blue eyes were shrewd. "What's this country have for a young girl?"

At that point, I hesitated. Dare I tell him anything? He knew this country better than any of us would ever know it, and given the proper clues could find such a treasure much sooner than we could. Yet if we were to find it, we must stay around and search . . . sooner or later he must know.

So I told him the story from the beginning, of our own meeting, of the death of Conway, and all that had transpired since. He listened, chewing on his old pipe.

"Figured as much," he said at last. He knocked out his pipe, tucking it away in his pocket. "Won't surprise you to know that's why I come here.

"I had the story from a Shoshoni. I heard it again from a Kansa. Never paid it much mind until I found myself a clue, an' that set me to huntin'."

"A clue?"

"Uh-huh. I found a strange cross cut into a rock. Looked like nothin' any Injun would make, so I set to figurin' on it."

"You've *found* the treasure?"

"No, sir. I surely ain't. Same time I figure I'm almighty close. It was huntin' about here that set me to findin' caves, an' I surely figured it would be hid away in one o' them. I found nothing no white man left. Bones, an' sech. I found enough of them."

"If we find it, it's for the girl. You understand?"

"That there gold belongs to who finds it, mister. It might be me. I hunted nigh onto ten year . . . off an' on."

"If you found it," I said, "you couldn't use it here. That would mean leaving all this. Leaving it behind forever."

He grunted, but said no more. More than an hour had passed while we talked, and I was wondering if my pursuers had moved along, but I said nothing.

We had been seated on rocks, talking. Restlessness was on me. While I sat here in relative comfort, my friends might be fighting for their lives.

"All right," he said, when I mentioned them, "we'll go see."

He led the way into a branch cave that inclined steeply up. He had cut crude steps into the limestone to make the climb easier. Suddenly the cave split and he led the way into the narrower passage of the two. We were climbing in a rough circle now, climbing what had evidently been a place where water had found a crack or weakness in the rock and had run almost straight down.

Above us there was light filtering down and we emerged on a steep hillside among several spruce trees that grew where there was scarce room for a man to stand. But just outside the entrance, which was under a shelf of rock and no more than three by four feet, was a flat rock.

Van Runkle seated himself. "A body can set here an' see whatever's in the bottom yonder. We're almost directly above the crack where you came into the cave, an' that there's the only blind spot for more'n a mile except for under the trees yonder."

I looked, and although I saw nothing of my friends, the first thing I did see was a jagged streak of white quartz on the rock wall opposite, just across the bottom and beyond the creek. From here I could see that creek, sunlight on its ripples. Hastily, I averted my eyes, not to seem too curious.

The wall along which I had run while following the dry watercourse that led to this cave had been of bluish stone, the jagged streak of quartz was opposite, and somewhere nearby Van Runkle had found a Maltese Cross on the rock.

Somewhere here, perhaps within a few yards, the treasure was buried or hidden.

"Nobody in sight," Van Runkle said, "and I surely can't hear anything. She's quiet as can be."

Suddenly something stirred up the valley, and then a deer

appeared. Behind it were two others. Tentatively they walked out on the grass and began to nibble.

Nothing happened; nothing disturbed them.

Down the valley I could see the bustling brown bodies of the marmots.

Across the way the slim white trunks of the aspen, under golden clouds of leaves, caught the sunlight. The grass of the meadow was green with patches of golden coneflower, the reds and pinks of wild rose and geranium.

"I'd like to own five thousand acres of this," I told him.

"What would you do with it?"

"Keep it. Keep it just as it is. I would not change it for anything under the sun. But it wouldn't have to be five thousand acres, just a piece of it that I could keep as it is now, fresh, clean, beautiful.

"There's no finer land than this before man puts a hand on it."

"You against men?"

"Of course not. Only men must *do*. It's in their nature to do, and much of what they've done is for the best, only sometimes they start doing before they understand that what they'll get won't be nearly as wonderful as what they had."

He grabbed my arm. "Look! An' be quiet!"

The marmots were scuttling. The deer turned their behinds to us and vanished into the brush, and there was for a moment stillness.

And into that stillness rode Rafen Falvey, and beside him was Lucinda. Behind them rode four men, armed and ready, and behind them Davy Shanagan and Jorge Ulibarri, hands and feet tied.

"Looks like he done taken the pot," Van Runkle said.

"No," I replied, "he has not. Not by a damned sight. I'm still holding cards in this game. Show me how to get down there, will you?"

SEVENTEEN

Yet for all my bold talk, when we reached the meadow, I had no idea of what to do or which way to go. Only that I must do something, and at once.

Where were the others? Had they been wiped out while I was in the deepest part of the cave and could not hear the shooting? Or had Falvey somehow captured Lucinda, Davy, and Jorge while they were separated from the group?

A moment only it required for decision. I could, of course, try to round up Degory, Solomon, and the others, yet in the meantime Davy, Jorge, and Lucinda might be put to the torture. I had no doubt that was intended, and no doubt that the reason Ulibarri and Davy were alive was simply to use them to compel Lucinda to tell what she knew . . . and they would never believe she knew so little.

Van Runkle stood beside me and I turned to him. "Is there a good camping place up the draw?"

He shrugged. "I reckon. Depends on judgment. The whole draw is a good place to camp. There's grass, fuel, and water. I don't figure they'll go far. If they reckon this is where it's at, they'll stay by."

True enough. And it was up to me to get my friends away, somehow to free them. If the others were alive, they would appear. If they were not, I would be foolish to waste time searching, especially as I was afoot. The fact that I was basically a walking man was a help. I was a rider, of course, but I always thought better and worked better on my feet.

"What d'you figure to do?" Van Runkle asked. His calm blue eyes studied me with curiosity.

"To get them away. I'll have to get close, see what the situation is, and then move.

"It's been a tradition in my family, when faced by enemies, to attack. No matter how many, no matter where. I had an ancestor named Tatton Chantry. He was a soldier in his time, and a fighting man always. He always said, 'Never let them get set. Think, look around, there's always someplace where they're vulnerable. Attack, always attack . . . and keep moving.'

"Good advice, if a body can do it."

"Well, I got nothin' to gain, but I'll sort of traipse along an' see what happens, but don't you go to dependin' on me. I'm like as not to disappear into the bresh come fightin' time."

We started off, walking fast toward the north. We kept along the edge of the woods, under the trees when a route offered itself, out at their edge when there was none.

My heart and lungs were acclimated to the altitude by now, and my condition was good. I moved out fast, keeping the Ferguson ready for a quick shot. The afternoon was well along and I had no doubt that in the leisure provided by a campfire they would try to learn whatever Lucinda knew.

Yet warily as I moved, my mind was busy with what could be done. To attack them head-on was out of the question. There were too many men and too many skilled woodsmen. So I must attack them where they were vulnerable, create confusion, and then somehow get their prisoners away. It was rather too much to expect of myself, but when one begins there is a certain impetus given by the fact of beginning, and I kept going.

Possibly because I had no idea of what else to do.

Being the man I was, eternally questioning not only my

motives but those of others, even as I moved forward my mind
asked questions and sought answers.

I suspect what I was doing would be called courageous. If I
rescued them, it might even be considered an heroic action,
but was it? Was I not conditioned by reading, by hearing, by
understanding what I *should* do?

To simply sit by was worse than to do, for then I should have
no idea of what was happening, of how my destiny was being
influenced by people over whom I had no control.

The sunset was spectacular. The sky streaked itself with rose
and the region of the sun became an indescribable glory. All
my life I have used words, and yet I find times when they are
totally inadequate.

So it was now, and not only because of the backlight left by
the sun, which had vanished beyond the mountains, but because
I had come upon Rafen Falvey's camp.

There was no attempt at concealment. Obviously he was not
worried about Indians, which indicated he was rather a fool. It
was, I assumed, an instance of his arrogance. One hates Indians or loves them, tries to understand them or simply guards
against them, but one never takes them for granted.

Of course, he had a motive for display. He wanted me, and
he wanted whomever he did not have. His idea was to lure us to
approach . . . which meant he probably had pickets posted
rather well out.

I stopped, Van Runkle still trailing me at a little distance.

Falvey had not one fire going, but three. Men moved in the
vicinity of the fires. I was a hundred yards or so from the camp,
and that I could see.

The mountain here sloped steeply down, the side covered
with trees. Undoubtedly at least one man was stationed there
where he could see anyone approaching the camp as the inter-
loper came between the watcher and the fires. It was likely
that one or more men would be stationed in the bottom itself,
one out in the grass, another in the creek bed.

My eyes grew accustomed to the deeper darkness, and I
could see that there was nothing in the next twenty feet, so I
moved up. A few more discreet moves and I was able to

distinguish faces in the company about the fire, and see where
the horses were kept in a rope corral beyond it.

A part of my problem was solved. I had to create confusion
and hit them where it would hurt most, and the answer was
obvious—their horses.

Without horses, existence in this country was virtually impossible. And without their horses they could carry no treasure,
nor could they escape. If their horses were scattered, they
must scatter in search of them.

Van Runkle now edged close. "What you aimin' to do?"

"Stampede their horses."

"Uh-huh. If'n you can get close enough, and if'n you can cut
that rope."

Crouched among the rocks, we watched the camp. The fires
were high, and they were cooking. The smell of food reminded
me of how hungry I was, but there would be no time for that
now. The camp was in a scattered grove of trees near the
stream, a poor place for defense, yet a good place to hold the
horses. From their disposition, they must believe no Indians
were in the vicinity.

"Is there a cave? Somewhere I can hide? I mean if I get her
away from them, we'll have to run."

Van Runkle hesitated. Obviously he had no desire to surrender his secrets, and he alone knew where the entrances of the
caves were hidden. But by some good fortune I had won him at
least partially to my side. "There's a cave up yonder." He
pointed up the slope and behind the camp. "It ain't part of my
lot so far's I know, but she's deep. There's some holes back in
yonder, so I'd not get too far in, if I was you. You'll find it right
behind some spruce with a half-peeled log lyin' in front."

Well, it was a help. I disliked the idea of using an escape
hatch I had not tested, but there was no remedy for it. If I was
fortunate enough to get the rope cut and the horses stampeded, I would have to get away at once before they scattered out
and found me.

The night was growing cold. I watched the fire with longing,
and then began my furtive crossing of the meadow between my
position and the belt of trees along the creek.

Somewhere out in the open there would be a picket, a man

sitting or lying down and waiting just for me. With luck I could pass far behind him. With no luck, I would be heard and shot without a chance.

Fortunately, the wind was picking up, and with leaves stirring and branches rustling, my movements might pass unnoticed. Carefully, I edged out of the trees, turned to grip Van Runkle's hand, and then I was committed.

Kneeling at the edge of the grass, I peered off in the direction I must travel. Roughly three hundred feet, but during all of that time I would be exposed. I felt strangely naked and alone.

I had no experience of war, and at an age when many young men had encounters with Indians, I had been studying in Europe and America. What in God's name was I doing here, anyway? Why had I ever left the east? And why was I taking such risks for a girl whom I scarcely knew?

Easing out to full length, my rifle across my upper arms, I squirmed out upon the grass, walking myself forward with my elbows. On my left I could hear the murmur of voices at the fires but could distinguish no words.

My body length . . . again . . . I crawled on. Sweat beaded my brow despite the chill wind. The earth was cold beneath me; the grass felt stiff and old. Leaves in the trees rustled, and I crawled on. Glancing back, I saw I was at least a third of the way out . . . at any moment I could come upon a sentry.

The thought occurred to me that I was in no position to defend myself if attacked, nor to attack myself. To accomplish anything I must rise, then strike, and it might be too late. Sliding my left hand down, I slipped off the thong that held my knife in its scabbard and drew it, then I took it in my teeth, the haft toward my right side.

It seemed silly and melodramatic, for I had seen old pen drawings of pirates carrying their knives so when boarding ships and using both hands in the process. But with the knife in my teeth, I had no need to rise, only to seize it and strike. I think it saved my life.

Inching forward, I fought down an impulse to rise and run for the trees, and held to my original pace, moving as silently as possible. Holding my head down, I suddenly felt the need to look up, and did.

Not three feet from me was a guard sitting cross-legged on the grass. At the instant I saw him, he saw me.

A moment we stared. He started to move, opening his mouth to yell, and in that instant I grabbed my knife by the hilt and swung it left to right, a wicked slash.

He had leaned slightly forward as one will do when starting to rise, and my backward slash was with all my strength. I held a knife of the finest steel, with an edge like a razor, and it cut deep and back.

The knife finished its cut and he was still trying to rise and draw his own knife when my hand came back. Making no effort to reverse the knife, I swung my arm in a mighty blow and struck him on the temple with the end of the hilt. He grunted and collapsed forward onto the ground, and then, in a panic, I was up and gripping rifle in one hand, bloody knife in the other, I ran.

At the trees, I drew up, not wanting to smash into them, and skidded to a halt.

All was quiet. Looking back, I could see nothing at all. Crouching, I slid my knife hilt deep into the earth and withdrew it, to cleanse it of blood. Rising, I slid into the trees and began working my way toward the corral.

There was little time. What I would do must be done at once, for soon they would change guards or call out to them and the missing one would be discovered. Soundlessly, I moved through the trees toward the fire.

Twenty feet back from the rope, I stopped. The horses had sensed me and were restless. I could see past their ears, for I was on somewhat higher ground, and in the camp I could see men eating, lying around, one man cleaning a rifle.

At first I saw nothing of Davy, Jorge, or Lucinda, and then I did. Lucinda was near to me, seated at the base of a tree, tied hand and foot. Falvey was near her. Beyond, and across the fire, I could see Shanagan. His hands appeared to be tied behind him. I couldn't spot Jorge.

No chance to get to Davy, but she was close. So were the horses. So far nobody had noticed their uneasiness. Stepping down through the trees, my hand found the encircling rope. A quick slash of the knife and it fell apart.

One of the horses jumped and snorted; the others bunched quickly. I ran at them, cutting the rope in another place and suddenly letting out a wild whoop.

They started to mill, then lunged and ran. A few of them hit the loosened rope and went through it and into the camp on a dead run. Men scattered. I saw one knocked down. The running horses plunged through the fire, out the other side of the camp, and into the darkness. The others milled, then when I whooped again, they ran.

I was within a dozen feet of Lucinda. Grabbing her by the collar, I lifted her bodily to her feet, and risking cutting her, I made a quick slash at the ropes at her ankles, then at her wrists.

A gun roared, almost in my ear it seemed, and a bullet struck the aspen near me and spat bark and stinging slivers into my face. Turning quickly, I shot from the hip, aiming at Falvey who had been knocked down by a horse as he started to rise. My shot missed, hitting a man just beyond him.

Sliding my knife into its scabbard, I grabbed at Lucinda's arm and ran. At almost the same moment, a rifle bellowed from across the way and a man running at me with a hatchet dropped in his tracks.

Suddenly I was in the darkness, running up through the trees. Behind me were shots, yells, then more shots. Somebody was staging a minor war back there, but there was no time to look.

Scrambling up through the trees, the slope was steep. Letting go of her hand, I used my hand to pull myself up by grasping tree trunks and limbs, as she did.

Somewhere up here, there was a cave, but there was not one chance in a million I could find it now, not in the dark with men searching for me. Coming out on a ledge, pausing to gasp for breath, I fumbled with the reloading of my Ferguson, made it, then started on.

We hurried along the face of the slope, moving southward, climbing a little, then back toward the north on a kind of switchback path or game trail.

Down below the shooting continued. I heard a shrill Indian yell, then the *bang* of another rifle. We climbed on, coming out in a small meadow.

Lucinda pulled on my sleeve. "Ronan . . . Mr. Chantry, I've got to stop. I . . . I can't run another step!"

We moved into the trees at the edge of the meadow and sat down on a log. She was not the only one who was all in. My breath was coming in ragged gasps and there was pain in my side.

Feeling for my knife, I slipped the loop back over the guard to keep it from slipping out.

I stood up. Behind us was a grove of aspen, before us what might be a trail used by Indians or buffalo or elk. "We must go," I said, and she got up.

The shooting down below had ceased. Soon they would be coming for us, and we had no place to hide.

EIGHTEEN

Yet I waited. I was tired of running and hiding. Slowly but steadily, anger had been building within me. Contemplation fits me better than rage. I am prone to consider before acting, and to take decisive action only when there is no other course. So far I had been guided by some instinct, some atavistic memory from warlike ancestors who had preceded me.

Now I no longer wished to escape. I wanted to fight. But beside me I had a girl to consider. Lovely as she was, intelligent as she was—and I have always preferred intelligent women—I wished for the moment she was elsewhere. A man going into a fight for his life should have to think of nothing else; his attention should not be for the minute averted.

There had been a lot of shooting below and I could only guess that my friends had appeared . . . my friends, or some Indians. If the former, I should join them; if the latter, I had another reason for hiding.

Van Runkle had mentioned a cave . . . but how to find it in the dark?

Turning to Lucinda, I asked, "Can you be still? As a ghost?"

"Ghosts rattle chains. Is that what you mean?"

"This is no time for levity. I want you to be still, to sit down in those trees yonder, and if somebody comes within inches, you are not to move . . . do you hear?"

"Yes."

"Very well, then. Into the trees with you."

There was a good stand of spruce, dark and close growing, and the log on which we sat was a good landmark, smooth as it was and white in the moonlight, and the moon would soon be up.

"What are you going to do?"

"Your uncle had some twenty men with him. He has fewer now . . . I think no more than sixteen or so. I'm going out to clip the odds a little more."

"You'll be killed. You're a scholar. Those men are vicious . . . unprincipled."

"And I'm principled. That, I suspect, places me at a disadvantage, and yet I'm not so sure that it does. At the moment I'm very much guided by several principles, and the first one is the desire to survive. The second one my family has used with some success. They believe in attack."

"You'll be killed. You're no match for such men."

It irritated me. Why do pretty women have the faculty of irritating? Almost as if they were trained for it. And, of course, they are. When one is irritated, one is not blasé. One must be interested or involved.

"You're mistaken. Socrates was a soldier, and a good one. So was Julius Caesar, and the playwright, Ben Jonson. There have been many."

She stood straight, looking into my eyes. "Sir, I do not want you hurt. I do not want you killed."

"Of course not. How could I help you obtain your treasure if I was dead? But I shall not be. Sit in those trees, and for God's sake, be still!"

Abruptly, I moved away from her. The moon was rising, and already it was growing lighter. Her doubt of my ability irritated me even more. I did not know who had attacked them after the horses were stampeded, but I knew that I had to carry the fight to them. Moreover, I must, if possible, free Davy and Jorge . . . if they yet lived.

There was silence upon the land. The aspens stood sentinel still in the moonlight, their golden coiffures shimmering slightly, gently, under the most delicate touch of the night air.

Down in the bottom, no fire glowed. No sound arose to meet me. There was a faint smell of woodsmoke from the extinguished fires, a dampness rising from the stream, and no other thing to disturb or impress itself upon the night.

Not only Lucinda's doubt rankled. There was also the quite obvious contempt of Rafen Falvey to spur me on. She doubted me capable of meeting him face-to-face, and he would have laughed at the idea.

When I had gone some three hundred yards, I squatted on my heels and listened. The stream rustled over its rocks, the aspens danced and whispered golden secrets to the moon. I heard nothing . . . and then I did.

Breathing. Someone breathing quite hard, a hoarse, rasping kind of breathing as someone after running. No. Someone hurt . . . someone wounded.

Listening, I placed the sound. Moved ever so gently. The breath caught . . . gasped. I edged closer. I could smell wet buckskin . . . then a low moan.

Was the sound familiar? I started to move, then some instinct brought my eyes up. The dark figure of a man was standing not four feet from me, and as I glimpsed him, I saw the spark leap as he pulled the trigger. Throwing myself aside, I shoved up the Ferguson and fired . . . not two inches from his body. The flash of his gun blinded me, and bits of powder stung my cheek, and then he was falling, falling right at me.

Almost automatically my fingers were fumbling with the reloading of my rifle. Dark as it was under the trees, my fingers felt true, and the gun was loaded, ready.

Again there was a low moan, then a whisper, "Scholar?"

It was Davy Shanagan.

Quickly, I moved to him. "Davy! Who did I shoot?"

"Don't . . . know."

"Are you hit hard?"

He took my hand and guided it to his side. There was a lot of blood. A lot too much. And nothing to do with. There was my kerchief. Taking that off I packed some damp moss into the wound, then my kerchief, and tied it in place with his thick leather belt.

"Lie still," I whispered. "Are you armed?"

"Knife. Rifle . . . empty."

Charging his Kentucky, I placed it beside him, then edged over to the man I had shot. Moonlight had reached his side. He wore a beaded belt that I did not know. I found his pistol and loaded it, then his rifle. The rifle I left with Davy, and tucking the extra pistol into my belt, I eased myself away into the brush.

The two shots could not have gone unnoticed. Obviously two men had fired, and somebody was probably dead. Whoever else was out there had no way of knowing who.

Working closer and closer to the camp, I soon saw my efforts were wasted. It was deserted. One lone horse stood out on the meadow, cropping grass, but the others had scattered, as had the people. The woods would be full of them, and somewhere Jorge Ulibarri was also, perhaps safe, perhaps dead, perhaps wounded, and needing help as Davy had.

Yet the futility of my efforts became obvious. In the darkness I could not tell friend from enemy, nor could I hope to find them, scattered as they were. Slowly, I worked my way back to Davy. He was still there, sleeping now.

Edging back beside him, I waited, listening. To stay with him or return to Lucinda? Reason told me she was safe, but it also told me Davy was sleeping and there was no more I could do to help him for the time. I decided to return.

Fifteen minutes it must have taken me to go the last hundred yards, and I am a good judge of time. The log with the bark scaled away lay white like a fallen temple column in the moonlight. I went into the trees. No Lucinda.

I could not believe it.

I listened, and heard no breathing. I spoke softly, and had no answer. I felt about, and touched nothing.

Lucinda was gone.

I had told her to stay where she was, and she had not done so. My irritation changed to anger, then to fear. Suppose she had been taken? Suppose Rafen Falvey had found her, or some of his men?

Crawling to where I had left her sitting, I felt all around . . . nothing.

And then my hand touched a knife. My fingers explored it in the darkness. Almost no guard . . . single edge. She had no knife that I had ever seen, and this was a skinning knife.

Someone had been here. She had been taken . . . but where?

There had been no outcry. In the silence of the night I could have heard it for a great distance.

Easing back into deeper shadow, I settled myself to wait for daybreak. To crawl around now would only disturb what sign was left, and there was nothing I could do, either to fight or run, until the day came again.

I thought of deliberately building a fire. It would probably call some of them to me, friends or enemies . . . but the problem was to know one from the other in the darkness. So I huddled tight against the bole of a spruce, under the dark, down-bending branches, and waited.

It was very still. The small sounds of the night seemed only to make greater the silence. Somewhere an owl spoke mournfully across the moonlit meadow, a bird ruffled its feathers nearby, a pine cone dropped, whispering through the needles, then falling to the ground.

Under the spruces it was very dark. I sat, rifle across my knees, listening and waiting. Alone in the night there are many sounds to hear, sounds always present but only heard in moments of stillness and waiting. How often, I thought, men had waited like this. The Greeks, concealed in their wooden horse outside the walls of Troy, must have heard such sounds as they waited. Would the Trojans accept the bait? Would they leave the horse where it was? Draw it inside as booty? Would they destroy it? Set it afire? The Greek soldiers had only to wait, to hope, and to remain absolutely silent.

Now I could see the fires down below were not as cold and dead as I believed. I could see red coals, like the eyes of beasts, waiting.

Not far away was Davy Shanagan. Had my quick treatment helped him? Had the bleeding stopped? Long ago Irish soldiers at the Battle of Clontarf had used moss to stop the bleeding of their wounds, so perhaps my reading of history had taught me something after all.

What had happened to Lucinda? Why had she not stayed where I left her?

Dawn was going to bring many things to a climax with so many armed men in so brief a space. I must sleep. Even if only a little. And if I was inclined to snore, I hoped on this night I would not.

When tomorrow came, there would be much to do. Get those of our group that survived together again. Find Lucinda, get the treasure, if treasure there was, then escape.

To achieve this we must have some freedom of action, which meant freedom from attack. Hence, I must locate the enemy and move against him in such a way that he must defend himself. I must immobilize him for a time, at least.

He had lost his horses by my first action. If he had recovered them, or some of them, I must act to disperse them once more. What was it Sun Tzu had said in 496 B.C.? *Speed is the essence of war. Take advantage of your enemy's unreadiness, move by unexpected routes, and attack unguarded spots.*

Well . . . if possible. And in the morning.

I went to sleep.

Within me was wariness . . . fear, if you like. My eyes opened upon a cold light, the gray, dim light before the sunrise. Lying still, I listened and heard nothing. Slowly, group by group I began to flex my muscles, pumping blood into them that my actions upon rising would be quicker. Carefully, I sat up.

A quail called . . . another answered.

Wiping the Ferguson clean of dew, I crept away from the bole of the tree to a better view. First I swept the area with a quick glance, then a more searching one. Then I directed my attention toward where Davy lay, but could see nothing of him, which was as it should be.

Rafen Falvey would try to assemble those men who remained with him. I believed he had lost at least four, but there had been further shooting, and the numbers might have been trimmed still more.

First, Lucinda.

Easing from my cover after a careful study of my surroundings, I went back toward the place I had left her. The log where we had rested was there.

Getting to my feet, I looked all around. Our tracks were plain enough, but she was gone.

A stir in the brush across from me and my Ferguson came level at waist height. Then a man emerged from the brush and it was Cusbe Ebitt. Behind him was Heath.

"They're movin'," Ebitt said. "Falvey has a skirmish line started up the slope . . . maybe two hundred yards back. Looks like they're aimin' to sweep the woods clean."

"Where are the others?"

"Search me. Ain't seen anybody but Isaac in hours. Where's she?"

My explanation was brief. Turning suddenly, the log came into my range of vision again. What was it Van Runkle had said? Something about a bare log, the bark fallen off . . . the cave was behind it, up the hill somewhat.

Beckoning them, I went into the trees. We worked our way up, and in low tones I explained what we were looking for. If we could hide in the cave, and then attack after they had passed. *There!* Under an aspen, clearly cut into the earth, the right side of a heel print—the corner of the heel, the line of the side, and a slight bit of the curve at back. A small sign, but sufficient. Lucinda had come up the slope then, and through the trees in the darkness. Why?

Looking ahead, I saw nothing but the slim columns of the aspens, a few young spruce growing in their shelter, and a crisscrossing of fallen trees. The slope was steep. The light was better now.

A camp-robber jay was keeping us company on the lower branches. Once we heard a faint sound and saw an elk moving away, just vanishing.

The trees thinned out. Before us was a rocky face, some broken, fallen rock on the ground, and in the sandy soil near the cliff face another track, a moccasin track of a wide foot, toeing out somewhat.

Van Runkle! We followed on and found Lucinda's track, well defined, again.

Van Runkle had Lucinda. I said it aloud and Isaac looked over at me. "Who is he?"

Explaining, I added, "He's been looking for the treasure, too. And he means to have it."

"We'd better find 'em then, an' almighty quick. You can't tell about a man like that."

We started again, searching for the cave, following the tracks.

And startled by this discovery, we forgot what we should have remembered.

Rafen Falvey and his men were coming up behind us.

NINETEEN

I t was a moment of carelessness that saved us.

They were still a good thirty yards off and most of them were among the trees when one of them stepped on a dry branch. It cracked, and I turned more swiftly than I have ever turned, and dropping to one knee, I fired.

The bullet took the first man high in the chest. Ebitt was a dozen feet to my right, and at the crack of the dead branch, he dove into the brush. Isaac, only an instant behind me, fired also.

It was point-blank range and I believe they had not seen us for they were slow in returning our fire. Isaac went into the trees only a step behind me, and the crack of Ebitt's rifle from the brush caused another man to reel and fall. He scrambled up and ran, however, injured but not seriously. But our fire made them all take to the brush.

Once under cover, we scrambled to find the cave, which must be within a few yards of us. Oddly enough we passed its opening several times before we saw it, and then it was Isaac who glimpsed it first. One after another we crawled in. The opening was large enough for one man only, and nobody was going to try to enter there with armed men waiting inside. That would not preclude them firing into the cave, however.

We looked around, straining our eyes against the gloom. The rear wall of the cavern was no more than thirty feet from the opening, but there was a wide gap to the left and several openings led off from it. Ebitt crouched, studying the sandy floor in the dim light.

"There's tracks," he said, "and they go into that one!"

We walked to the opening. There was a faint stir of cool air from the opening. "We'll need a torch," Heath commented. "Back from the opening, a body can't see nothing."

"Wait," I said, loading my Ferguson. One hand felt for my pistol, and it was there.

We could hear shouts and yells from outside, the sounds of men crashing in the brush. Heath moved closer to me. "Seen some small boot-tracks. Likely to be Lucinda's."

"All right," I said. "Look around, Isaac. You might find something for a torch. Others have come this way and they'd need light."

Suddenly I remembered. "Be careful! There may be a drop off!"

Their voices receded, and for the moment I was alone. The temperature of the cave was cool, but not unpleasant. Rifle in hand, I sat watching the circle of light that was the entrance. I was tired. For days I had been riding, running, climbing, and now it was reaching me. No sound came from outside. Had they gone away? Or were they sitting outside, waiting for us to appear? And where were the others? Where were Solomon, Bob, Degory, and Jorge?

Isaac returned. For several minutes I heard his feet coming along the passage before I saw him. "We've found some pine knots. Quite a store of them."

"Then we'll go."

He turned and I straightened up, stretching a little. The butt of the Ferguson touched the rock wall and I turned to look.

A Maltese Cross . . .

Chipped into the wall, and not recently, by the look of it. A Maltese Cross with one side of a cross bar longer than the other. Accident? Or intent?

No footprints in the sand led into that tunnel. I hesitated, staring into the blackness. From down the other passage, Heath called, "You comin'?"

"In a minute."

Van Runkle had warned of deep wells within this cave. Was it true? Or merely a means to prevent my wandering and searching?

I took a step into the blackness. The air was cool. It seemed to be dead air . . . or did I feel a ghost of movement? Another step, my hand upon the wall, my rifle point probing ahead of me.

Nothing. I took another step, and my foot kicked a small fragment fallen from the wall, or carried in on the mud of a boot. The stone hit something, then fell. A long time later I heard it hit, something far down below me, and then again, still farther. A still longer time, then a splash.

Very carefully, I stepped back, then turned and retreated into the dim light of the entrance cave. Was that where the treasure was? Or was it a deathtrap deliberately planned for the curious or the searcher after gold?

Enough for now. Somewhere Lucinda might need us, and her life was more precious than whatever gold there might be. I walked swiftly along the passage until I saw a glow of light ahead.

Isaac and Cusbe waited, both with lighted pine knots. Taking another from the goodly pile, I lighted it also and we started along the tunnel at a good clip. A hundred feet of slowly enlarging tunnel, then a vast room. But an opening was directly opposite and we crossed the room, seeing the scar of a footprint in the dripping from the rocks above.

When we had gone some distance, we saw light ahead. We smothered our torches, and stepping into the lead, I walked on.

We found ourselves in a roomy, pleasant cave. There were several bearskins about, one of them on a bench with other furs. And the first thing we saw was Van Runkle. He was seated on a skin-covered seat of some sort, with a shotgun in his hands, and he was watching us. Lucinda sat on the bearskin against the wall.

"Thank you for taking care of Miss Falvey," I said quietly. "It was good of you, sir."

His shrewd eyes appraised us. "Ain't said as I was," he replied. "Mebbe I'm a-holdin' her. Right nice filly, that one. Better'n a squaw."

"I agree. She's a handsome lass. And we, my friends and I, have taken it upon ourselves to find what she came here to get, and then to escort her to a place in civilization where she can live as a young lady should."

"Nice of you." He took his pipe from his mouth with his left hand. "Right nice. If'n I decide to let her go."

"And as one gentleman to another, I know you will. The young lady is far from home and relatives. Naturally she's frightened—"

"I am not!" She held her head proudly, her chin lifted a little. "I'm not afraid of him. He brought me here when I was cold and tired, and he's been very kind."

"Of course. Mr. Van Runkle and I have met before, and he is kind, and a gentleman, as I suggested.

"Now, sir, I think we had better think of getting out of here and continuing on our way. We must round up our horses, as we have far to go."

"You just stand right there where you be. You ain't goin' to cut much figger with a belly full of buckshot, and I got it to give you. Hayl bullets, some calls 'em. Well, whatever they call 'em, they're just as good at tearin' a man up."

"You might shoot," I said, "but we'd kill you. I have a rifle, as have these gentlemen with me. And no matter how much buckshot you throw my way, I'll still manage a shot. Believe me, I will.

"The mind is a powerful thing, my friend, and the will can complete a movement even when a man's dying. If you shoot, I'll kill you as well."

"Mebbe. An' mebbe you ain't got the guts for it."

I smiled at him. "Mr. Van Runkle, you may wonder why a man of my attainments has come west. I came west to die, sir. My wife and my child died back there in a fire. There are many fires in a land where candlelight and open fireplaces exist, and I lost all I loved.

"So you see, Mr. Van Runkle, I have the edge. I just don't give a damn!"

Lucinda was staring at me as if she had never seen me before.

Van Runkle scowled. There was a difference between facing a man who might be controlled by fear and one who was utterly careless, and my story had just enough truth in it for him to believe me. He had no wish to die, but you cannot bluff a man who simply does not care . . . and he was not prepared to gamble on the fact that I might be lying.

"Put the gun down, Van Runkle," I said quietly, "or shoot, but when your finger tightens on that trigger, you're going to take a slug right through the belly!"

Ebitt, who had entered the room with his gun muzzle lowered, now tilted his, as did Isaac Heath.

"Hell," Van Runkle said with disgust, "you just ain't got no humor! I didn't mean to shoot nobody! I got as much reason for stoppin' that Falvey feller as you uns have!" He put his shotgun down and stood up.

His gaze leveled at me. "You got nerve, young feller."

"It's not hard to be brave," I said, "when you just don't care."

Lucinda came over to us. I gestured with my gun muzzle. "Lead us out of here, Van Runkle, and you walk ahead." He started to pick up the shotgun. "No . . . we've guns enough. You walk on."

I picked up the shotgun. I still did not believe him a bad man. A dangerous one, yes. A man who might seek to take advantage of an opportunity that seemed to offer itself, but not a genuinely bad man. Nevertheless, while believing that, I was quite sure I was going to keep my eyes open and my gun handy so that no such opportunity should come upon him again. It was my job to see that he was not tempted.

The mountain was honeycombed with caves, as was the scarp where we now were. A thought occurred to me, and I mentioned it.

"Are the caves connected under the valley?"

"I figure so," he admitted, "although I never found a way. Mebbe it's under water. More'n likely it's all one big cave.

Miles of passages nobody ever looked into, not even me, and I seen more of these caves than even them old-time Injuns."

We emerged on a ledge, higher up on the mountain and among some cedars, wind-barbered spruce, and the like. Just above us was the shelf of the plateau of which the escarpment was the edge, and below the country was laid out as on a map, a clear view of a magnificent stretch of country.

How to locate our people? Neither Ebitt nor Heath had any suggestions. All we could do was explore, carefully, and hope we came upon them.

"The key to the situation is Rafen Falvey," I commented, to no one in particular. "If he was out of the way, I think the rest of them would break up and scatter out."

"You're dead right," Heath said grimly, "but how do you figure to be rid of him?"

"If he were whipped, decisively whipped, I think he'd lose most of his men. I propose to challenge him."

They stared at me, and I am quite sure they thought whatever good sense I'd had had abandoned me. Isaac Heath cleared his throat. "Now see here," he spoke reasonably, "you've been doing well out here. For a scholar, you're an almighty good rifle shot, and you've stood up well to the life, but have you ever really *looked* at Rafen Falvey?"

"That's quite a man," Cusbe commented. "He'll outweigh you forty pounds, he's a couple of inches taller, and I figure he's a whole lot meaner than you be."

Lucinda was watching me, and it irritated me to be considered less than Falvey before her. She was nothing to me . . . simply a girl I was helping through a bad time . . . nonetheless I liked not the belittling.

"He's somewhat taller, but I'm more solid than I look, and I doubt if he's more than twenty pounds heavier. As for being meaner . . . I'm not at all sure about that."

"Lay off him," Cusbe advised. "He'll kill you. The man moves like a cat. You've seen him in action. He's swift, sure, and never at a loss. He's a dead shot and good with a knife. How do you figure you could match him?"

"Knives, pistols, or fists," I said. "He can choose the weapons." I touched the knife at my side. "This is the finest steel ever made."

The fact that I was a bookish man led them to believe I might be less physical than they, but as a matter of fact I have always been uncommonly strong and agile. Strength of body was an inherited quality in my family, and my life had been an active one since boyhood. In Europe I had hiked, fenced, wrestled, and boxed, and had been considered an unusually skillful swordsman.

It was true that I had had few fights of any kind, but I came of a fighting stock, professional soldiers and fighting men, adventurers and seafaring men. If one is to judge from racehorses and hunting dogs, breeding counts for much.

"No use talkin' of it," Cusbe said. "Even if you two fit an' you whopped him, there's no reason to believe he'd hold to his word. That's a dangerous, treacherous man yonder, and nobody for a schoolteacher to face up to."

I was nettled . . . angry. "Many scholars have been men of uncommon strength," I said irritably. "Socrates, for example. He once threw Alcibiades and held him down, and Alcibiades was not only very strong, a noted athlete, but a young rowdy.

"Leonardo da Vinci could bend iron horseshoes with his hands, and Plato was a noted athlete before he became a teacher. Plato was actually a nickname, given him because of his broad shoulders."

"We ain't talkin' of them," Cusbe replied. "You just forget any such nonsense. That's a dangerous man, yonder. A fighter from wayback."

Perhaps I was a fool, but their objections only made me angrier. To meet Falvey and destroy him seemed the only immediate answer.

How long we had been underground I had not realized, but the morning sun was bright, dancing on the ripples of the stream far below. No man could have dreamed a scene more lovely or more peaceful. Looking up at the peaks, my heart felt good.

"You goin' down yonder?" Van Runkle asked.

"We are."

"You got no call to take me. I got no use for them down there, but I surely ain't goin' to 'em without me a *wee*-pon."

"You've weapons enough in those caves," I said. "Go get one of them. I've no wish to take a load of buckshot in the back."

"I'd not shoot you," Van Runkle protested, "but I set store by that gun. That's a gen-you-ine Henry Nock scatter-gun. They don't make them no better."

"You're right, sir. I had the good fortune to meet Mr. Nock in England when he was developing this gun. I'll care for it, and with luck, I'll return it to you. Now crawl into your hole and be off."

The Ferguson I slung on my back. For the moment the shotgun might be more useful. It was a powerful, double-barreled weapon, much superior to the long-barreled fowling pieces that preceded shotguns, some with barrels as much as six and one-half feet long, and cumbersome to handle.

We started forward. It was beautiful, it was serene, it was still, but somewhere down there, death awaited. Perhaps mine.

TWENTY

Pride can be a dangerous associate, and a thinking man should beware of it, for it can lead him into risks and troubles he would not otherwise endure. My friends as well as Lucinda doubted my ability to meet Rafen Falvey in anything like even combat, and the idea rankled.

Heretofore, I had considered myself a calm, intelligent human being, and all good sense told me that what I should now do would be to find the treasure, gather my friends about me, and get out of the country as fast as ever I could.

If we could get to our horses, there was a chance we might leave them completely behind, and reach the Mandan villages before they could come anywhere near. My common sense assured me this course of action was best, and as my anger cooled, I started out to bring it to completion. Yet irritation remained with me.

Cautiously we scouted toward the area where I had last seen Davy Shanagan. We found blood upon the leaves, the marks left by his body, but he was gone.

Crouching in the trees, we considered the situation. Plainly visible was the former encampment of Falvey's men, now

150

abandoned. One horse remained there, but I did not like the look of it.

"Bait," I said. "They must be waiting for us to come after it."

"We better light out an' find our horses again. If them Falvey men ain't found them, they'll be where we hid them after you went off up the slope that night and we decided to scoot when we heard Falvey's men go by."

"Where was that?"

"Neat little hollow in the hills, yonder. There's a spring, and a scattering of trees, good grass. Bob Sandy was to stay with our stock, him being in no shape to traipse over the country."

We backed off from the camp area. It was unlikely a horse would remain in an abandoned camp without reason. That it was picketed or somehow kept there seemed obvious.

We went back from the edge of the scarp and worked our way by game trails through stunted oaks, oak brush, and a few pines. Stopping from time to time to listen, we heard nothing. At the copse where the horses had been left, all was quiet. The horses were there, cropping grass or standing head to tail to swish flies from each other's noses. For some minutes we lay still, studying the situation.

There was no sign of life, but there easily could be somebody in the shadows at several points. And Bob should be there.

The shotgun I carried was growing heavy, and I wanted nothing so much as a chance to put it down, to drink some coffee, eat something, and then saddle up and pull out.

After a few minutes of observation when we saw no one, we descended into the hollow and saddled our mounts and the others as well.

It was an eerie feeling, and all of us had a sense of foreboding. Falvey was in the area, he had a good-sized force, and without doubt some at least had recaptured their horses. Undoubtedly they were expecting a move from us, just as we were from them.

To the east of the hollow, there was a thick stand of pines, and we led the horses into these and through them to a smaller but more easily defended hollow on the far side. There was fuel in plenty, and risking discovery, we made coffee and a meal.

Fitfully, we napped, taking turns at watching. As darkness came nearer, we knew a move must be made. I had been thinking about the Maltese Cross in the cave. Presumably there was another one outside as well, the one Van Runkle had found, but I could not be certain.

On the ground near me, I traced out a line showing the edge of the scarp and the mountain opposite, the location of the cave with the cross, and our own position. If I was not mistaken, we were not more than three hundred yards back of that cave in a southeasterly direction.

Choosing a tall, ragged pine standing on the rim of the scarp for a landmark, I sighted along a line from our position to that tree. About halfway to the pine was an outcropping of rock. Between there and here a small pine was a deadfall. I should be able to hold a true course even in darkness. I found a couple of pine knots loaded with pitch and put them in a convenient place.

Lucinda came over to me. "What do you plan to do?"

"Get the treasure and get out," I replied.

"Good!" she said quickly. "I want to go . . . even without it. Let's just *go!*"

She was silent for a moment, and then she said, "I'm afraid of him. I believe he'd willingly kill us all . . . everyone!"

Despite my bold wish to challenge him, I was not unafraid myself. That Rafen Falvey was a fighting man almost without peer was something we accepted. He was a bold, daring man who kept his crew of roughs in submission partly through fear and partly through sheer personality. Yet, stubbornly, I refused to admit defeat. I would have the treasure . . . then we would go.

The country around was deceptively calm. Nobody moved wherever we looked.

For the moment, we seemed secure, which is a dangerous feeling. At such times one becomes vulnerable, and we had no wish to be attacked. As I studied the terrain, looking not only for movement but for any suggestion of past movement, it seemed to me that the thing to do was to make one quick attempt to obtain the treasure, and then to get out of the country as swiftly as possible. Our main object was to protect

Lucinda, on this all would agree, and that meant getting away. Sandy, Talley, Kemble, Shanagan, and Jorge knew our destination and could follow, if they lived, and if we did.

Ebitt moved over to me, studying the country as I did. "Have you got an idea where the stuff is?"

"I think I know where it is."

"Well, you're one up on me. I surely don't."

Then I explained about the Maltese Cross in the cave. "I think the long arm of the cross was a deception . . . intended as a trap. I think the stuff is buried below it."

"Could be." Cusbe lighted his pipe. "I wish those boys would get to us. I fear for them . . . and for us."

"And I do. Shanagan was in bad shape."

We waited out the day, snatching bits of rest, letting the horses crop grass and store strength for the coming race across the plains.

The shadows lengthened. They were waiting as well as we, but with darkness there would be renewed activity, and suddenly I decided that now was the time to move, now in the last moments of light.

We mounted, and moved out, pointing across the grass toward the outcropping. Somewhere a quail called inquiringly into the stillness, but there was no other sound but our horses' hooves in the grass. At the outcropping, we drew up, merging our outline into the grayness of the rocks.

My rifle was over my shoulder on a sling, but the shotgun I carried in my hands. For a moment we were still, studying the edge of the woods, listening, waiting. There was no sound, yet I was worried.

"I believe they're waiting for us," I whispered to Heath. "I think they know where we are."

"Then there'll be a fight."

At the ragged pine leaning over the edge of the scarp, we drew rein. Swinging from the saddle, I handed the shotgun to Heath. "I'll go down alone. Do you stand by with Lucinda."

Before us lay the edge of the scarp, behind the open country we had crossed. Cusbe Ebitt swung to the ground, followed by Lucinda and Isaac. The position was not good, but there were a few low rocks, some brush, and a fallen tree. None were advantageously placed, but they offered slight shelter.

At this point, the scarp was all of sixty feet high, and I could but dimly make out what lay below. There were several possible routes down, and I chose what seemed the most simple.

Careful to dislodge no stone, I worked my way down, taking my time. There was no sound from above. At the bottom, all remained still. It was too good, and I did not like it. A broken tree I had taken as a marker was close by the opening, but I did not immediately move that way. Something was now stirring down on the bottom but I could make out nothing. It sounded like horses . . . several of them.

Carefully, I edged along, looking for the mark. The cave was near. Taking the Ferguson from my back, and checking the position of my pistol, I moved toward it.

Suddenly I was there, and I paused, drawing deeper into the shadows. All was at stake. I acted upon no knowledge, only a hunch, a feeling. Nor would I be permitted much time for searching. Even now my friends atop the scarp might be in danger of their lives. Indeed, they were at every minute they remained in this place.

The dark mouth of the cave yawned near me. What awaited within? Van Runkle? It was possible. He, at least, knew this spot, and the others could have discovered it. Scholarship would help me not at all, only muscle, nerve, swiftness of action, and luck.

How much had I changed in the weeks since I rode away from the Mississippi and started west? Or had the change not begun before that, when my wife died, and my son?

There were fires enough. Each year families died, homes were destroyed. Sparks from a fireplace, overturned candlesticks . . . there were many such accidents, and mine had been but one of these. My tragedy was but one among many, but to me it was the only one. To me my wife and son were not statistics, but the heartbeat of my life.

Had the change begun then? Or was there, actually, any change at all? Had not these feelings, these instincts, been lying deep within me? Holding myself still here beside a yawn-

ing black hole into which soon I must go, I found myself ready
to enter, ready and even anxious for what awaited within.

There had never been any of the cowardice in me that makes
men move in gangs to hunt other men. What fighting I had to
do I wanted to do with equal weapons, with even terms. Yet
the new wisdom I had acquired told me the enemy had no
such scruples.

Suddenly, ducking my head, I went through the entrance
into the dark coolness of the cavern. Flattened against the wall,
my back protected, I listened.

A moment I waited, holding my breath. The cave was cool,
still. I heard no sound, no breathing, no chafe of clothing
against a cave wall. I edged along, took a step, then another.
No light now . . . I must work in darkness. I had counted the
steps from the Maltese Cross to the cave mouth. Now I counted
them back . . . found the branch cave I sought. A few steps
too far now and I would plunge into that abyss . . . perhaps
hundreds of feet deep.

There had been a round rock on the floor within inches of
the cross. My toe touched it. Kneeling I felt of it, then felt
along the wall for the cross.

The long arm of the cross pointed toward the abyss, but I
was sure that was a trap or perhaps pure accident. I believed
the treasure was buried beneath the cross. With my fingers, I
probed the dust at the base of the cross.

Solid! My fingers felt for edges, and there were none, felt for
softness, and all was hard. The cave floor had been undisturbed
for years.

So there it was then. I had failed. It only remained for me to
return, to go back the way I had come, get Lucinda and ride,
trusting to my good companions to come when they could.
Heath and Ebitt agreed it was the thing to do.

But empty-handed?

My hands felt the wall, searching for cracks my touch might
find that sight had failed to perceive. There was nothing.

A Maltese Cross has two arms, either of which could point at
something, a bottom that could also be a pointer. But the top?
Suddenly I felt upward, reaching as high as I could . . .
nothing.

And I was a tall man, taller than most.

Yet my fingers did not reach the cave ceiling. Somehow I had believed it was low, just above my head. Now I knew that was an illusion of the darkness, as the cave went higher still. Crouching by the wall, I considered that.

I was well back into the cave, yet to see what lay above I must have a torch. They were close at hand, some pine knots that would burn well and throw a good light. It was unlikely that such a light could be seen outside the cave, yet from the mountain opposite, it was possible.

Minutes were passing. How long had I been gone?

Feeling for the pine chunks, I found them, also a section of log from which pine slivers had been broken. Suddenly I realized it would make a good footstool. I could stand upon it and reach higher. Edging it into position, I stood on it, balancing with my hands against the wall, then reached up.

My fingers encountered some sticky strings. A shiver went through me. I touched my fingers, which I had hastily jerked back. Not pitch, something slippery, wet. Moisture from a stalactite? No . . . there were no grains, no powdery-wet feeling.

What then?

Blood? . . . *Blood!* . . . But whose blood?

My hand went up again, again the wet finger, then buckskin . . . an arm, a fringed sleeve.

I must have a light. Feeling for flint and steel, I was stopped by a low moan.

Lighting a small sliver of the pitch pine, I stepped back on the log and held it up.

As my small light flared, the injured man's head turned.

"*Davy!* Davy Shanagan! How in God's world did you—?"

"Had to . . . hide. They were comin'. I crawled, found a hole up above. I crawled, and fell . . . maybe six, seven feet. Started bleedin' again. I tucked your moss in, finally got her stopped."

Holding up my hands, I got him under the armpits while he held the pine sliver. Then I eased him down to the floor of the cave.

"I'm better. Slept some."

"I was hunting the treasure, Davy. Had no idea you were up there."

"Figured as much. Well, you needn't hunt no longer. It's there."

I stood up. "Davy . . . you mean it?"

"Sure. When I crawled in the crack up there, I fell right atop of it. She's there, all right. At least there's four hide cases up there . . . rotted some. One of them busted when I fell."

"Davy, the treasure will have to wait. I've got to get you to Ebitt and Heath. They're just—"

"You don't need to do that, Chantry. A bullet will take care of him, and another for you!"

It was Rafen Falvey.

I left the cave floor in a plunging dive with all the thrust of my legs behind it, and I hit him just below the knees.

TWENTY-ONE

H e fell back, out of the cave, and we came up together. His men were waiting outside and I prayed they had heard nothing. They started to close in, but the click of a rifle hammer stopped them.

"We got some rifles out here"—it was Solomon Talley speaking—"and we don't much mind who we shoot. You men just step back and let them be. If they've something to settle, let them have at it."

Falvey laughed. "You'd fight *me*?" His amusement was obvious. "Schoolteacher, you're more of a fool than I suspected."

"Possibly. But that's something we'll have to discover, isn't it?"

"What weapons then, schoolmaster, do you choose?"

"Whatever you like. I'd prefer to whip you with a weapon you've chosen. Shall it be hand-to-hand?"

He laughed again. "Scholar, in my pirate days I was considered the greatest hand-to-hand fighter among all who flew the black flag. Why not choose again?"

"Afraid?"

His laughter wiped out on the instant. "Afraid? Of *you*? Why, you contemptible—!"

"What is it then? Are you choosing name-calling, Falvey? Is that your weapon? Only a loud mouth?"

"Hand-to-hand, then. Fists and as you will. Take to the knife when it pleases us."

"And no interruptions, gentlemen!" That was Heath speaking, so they were here, too. All of us, I hoped.

He struck, suddenly, savagely. An inch or two lower and he might have knocked me out, but there was a quick, partial move to evade on my part and the fist took me on the cheekbone, a wicked blow that staggered me, shook me to my heels, and all I could do was duck my head and close with him.

He threw me promptly, over his hip and into the dust, and then he dropped, a knee ready for my belly, but I rolled over swiftly, unexpectedly for him, and we both came up fast. But that time I was first to land. A stiff, straight punch to the teeth, that shook him to his heels and then we were fairly at it.

He was the taller man, with the longer arms, and he was heavier, but since a boy I had hiked and rambled in the woods, had swung an axe, and growing older had tumbled and wrestled with other lads. In Europe I had fenced and boxed. Often I had sparred with Daniel Mendoza, one of the greatest pugilists of the time, hence I was not quite the innocent they believed me to be.

He smashed me in the face with both fists, and I put a solid one to his ribs. He struck me again, on the ear, then on the chest, but I put another one under his heart. We sparred briefly, and then were at it, hammer and tongs, both fists flying. He landed more punches, and for a time the harder ones, but I put three more stiff ones into his midsection, and one to the face.

He backheeled me and we both fell. Again he tried for my groin with the knee, but I smashed up with both feet as he came down and kicked him off. He hit the ground on his backside, but we both came to our feet together.

"So, Scholar, you can fight, too?"

"A little," I said, "but I am not the greatest hand-to-hand fighter under the black flag."

He came in swiftly, struck at my face with a jab of his left that I parried, hitting him again over the heart.

He laughed at me. "Nothing but ribs there, you'll do no good. They're iron."

I feinted toward his face, stepped in and smashed another one to the same place, and then as we clinched, I hit him twice more in the same spot. He threw me off, angry now. Struck me in the face. I went under his next blow with a straight, hard right to the body.

The blow caught him coming in and I knew I had hurt him. He smashed me in the face with an elbow, over and back, and I butted him under the chin, not minding the rough stuff, stamped on his instep, and butted him again. He broke free, cut my face with a right, and took two solid ones to the belly, and they hurt. He backed away, circling, trying to decide what to do with me. Finally he came in, I ducked one punch, but the second caught me fairly on the chin and I was knocked down. Dazed, I started to get up. He kicked at my face and I had barely the chance to turn my head. The kick cut the side of my head and knocked me over into the dust. He jumped to come down on my stomach with both heels, but I jerked both knees up and kicked out. My double kick caught him coming down and spilled him. He fell near me, grabbing at my face with his clawed hand, reaching for my eyes.

Panic-stricken, wild with fear, I struck his hand away and scrambled up. He was wild now, and he came at me swinging both fists. I was driven back and back, his fists hammering at my face, and there was no chance to get set, no chance to ward off the blows. I went to my knees and his own eagerness carried him on. He half fell and we both got up, but he was on me like a tiger. I could not get a blow into him, only keep my elbows in close and my hands close to my face. Had he taken a bit more time he might have had me then, for the very ferocity of his attack swept me back. I had boxed much, but had never fought anyone like him, and he was relentless. Finally in sheer desperation I ducked my head against his chest and smashed both hands to the body.

He shoved me off, chopped a short one to my chin, and I shook it off and went in, swinging both fists to his body, and then lifting a right in a furious uppercut that caught him on the chin. He staggered, and his knees buckled, and as he started to fall, his hand went to his knife.

It caught the haft and he swung the blade in a wicked slice at my belly that had it reached me would surely have ripped me open from side to side. My own blade came out, but this was something at which I had my own skill. He came in, but I was ready, my knife held low for the soft parts of the body. He slashed again but I parried it with my own knife and his blade slid off it and away. I stepped in to cut him, and his knife came back and up. Too late I saw it coming, tried to evade the trap he had set for me. The knife was coming up hard for my groin, and there was but one thing I could do. Using his shoulder as a balance point, I turned sharply on the ball of my left foot, spinning clear around. The blade missed . . . or seemed to . . . and I fell backward to the ground.

He turned sharply to face me, knife ready to kill. Cold sweat broke over me. For the first time I really realized what I was in for. In the turmoil of movement and fighting, somehow there had been no realization that this was a fight to the death. Subconsciously the knowledge had been there, of course. In that moment of looking up at him, his eyes blazing, his face twisted with ferocity, I knew I wanted to live.

He came at me. The point of my blade to him, I dropped my other hand to the earth beside me. How to get up without that terrible moment of rising off-balance and vulnerable. He circled and I turned my feet toward him, turning clockwise, and then he stepped in.

Instantly I hooked my toe behind his ankle and kicked hard with my heel for his kneecap.

It should have broken his leg, but he threw himself backward to the ground and my heel glanced harmlessly off his shin, and then we were both up, facing each other.

There was no contempt now, no fear, only desperation, eagerness for the kill, and the knowledge on his part as on mine that all the chips were down.

There was sudden confidence in me. I had survived this long, I had met him on even terms, and it was he who first resorted to the blade. And the knife I held in my hand had

been long in my family. The knife from India . . . long since
. . . how much history there was to that knife! A history of
many Chantrys, and of others, men who had used that blade of
the finest steel ever created.

Confidence welled up within me. With this knife, this blade—
He came at me then, and he came to kill.

He was quick. His knife flicked out like a snake's tongue and
I felt the bite of it in my arm. Not deep, but a few more of
those . . . Many knife fighters used just that tactic, flicking
slashes with the point of the blade, never getting too close,
always difficult to reach, and in a matter of minutes a man
might be bleeding from two dozen gashes, and growing steadily weaker.

Yet he was not playing for time. He wished to make me
cautious, less of a threat to himself while he sought the opening
he wanted. He circled, always ready. His knife blade came
again, and my parry was an instant too late. Another tiny slash,
blood showing in two places on my knife arm now.

I let my arm shrink back, closer to my body. His eyes flicked
to mine and purposely I feigned weakness, circling away. He
feinted, and I stepped back so sharply that I stumbled. He was
still not sure, but his blade flicked again. That time I parried
the blow successfully, yet feigned clumsiness.

Suddenly stepping in, he drove a hard blow at my eyes,
which I parried, and for a moment, our knives locked tight by
the strength of our muscles, we were face-to-face.

"Now I'm going to kill you, Scholar." He said it softly,
smiling a little.

"Yes?" I said, then gave ground as if weakening, yet keeping
my knife tight to his.

He disengaged suddenly, feinted a thrust, and I countered
as if my right arm were stiffening or weakening. He circled,
still wary, watching for his moment. It came suddenly.

My point fell a little, and then as if fighting weakness, I
raised my arm higher and wider to the right, out of line with
my body. Trapping him though I was, his attack was so sudden, so swift that he nearly nailed me.

He lunged, thrusting for my abdomen. Only the swift turn of

my body saved me and a slight deflecting blow with my left palm against his right arm. The thrust went past, ripping my shirt front. Instantly my own blade cut down. My hand turned thrusting down and in from the thumb side of the hand. Too late he saw it coming and tried to knock down my hand. His blow missed and my blade stabbed home, into the solar plexus and to the hilt.

He gave a grunt as my fist struck his body, my left hand went to his shoulder and pushed him hard away, the knife coming free.

Blood followed, coming through the deep stab wound, reddening his shirt, covering the front of his body. He stepped after me, and I retreated. I had no desire to stab him again, and no wish to be stabbed, and no time was left to him.

"You damned bloody—!" He went to his knees, and I walked to the Ferguson and took it up. Thrusting the knife deep into the soil, I withdrew it and thrust it into its sheath.

My rifle came level at hip height. "Take him," I told them, "and get out!"

There were other rifles around me, all ready. They looked at their leader, still on his knees and bleeding, and they looked at our guns.

"To hell with him!" one of them said roughly. "There ain't no treasure anyhow." The others nodded, talking among themselves. I waited for Falvey to tell them about our find. But he said nothing. Gesturing with my rifle, I motioned them away. They turned in their tracks and walked toward their horses, still talking against Falvey.

Falvey himself had sunk back on his heels, holding the wound with his hand. "Damn you, Scholar," he spoke calmly now, "you tricked me. What books did you read, anyway?"

"I'm sorry. You left me no choice."

"Thought it would come in a night at sea," he mumbled, "never like this . . . not here."

"Isaac"—I spoke without turning my head—"get Lucinda to the horses. That bunch may change their minds and come back."

Reluctantly, Heath moved back, and Ebitt and Kemble helped

Davy. Solomon Talley said, "I'll cover you from the rocks. Come when you're ready."

Yet I stood there, curiously reluctant to leave. The man was dying, and I did not want to see him go alone, here in the gray light before the dawn.

He looked at me. "You're a good man, Scholar, a good man. Believe me or not, I've known a few." He jerked his head toward the way his followers had gone. "Rabble," he said, "a thieving lot. That's the trouble with crime." He smiled. "The company's bad." He coughed, holding himself against a spasm of pain. "Ah, Scholar! What a team we'd have made!"

"Can I do anything for you?"

"You did it, friend. You did it with that scurvy blade. It's all you can do for any man."

He coughed again and I thought for a moment he would fall. "Go on with you, man. I need no pity. Let me die alone . . . it's the way I've lived."

Talley called from the scarp above and I backed away and then climbed the rocks. When I stood on the edge, I looked down. The light was graying and I could make him out dimly. He had fallen over on his side . . . a bad man, but a man of courage for all that.

The men were taking the last of the treasure from the opening through which Davy Shanagan had fallen when I reached the top. Davy had pointed out the way and they had crept down a slanting break in the scarp's edge to reach the entrance. Sacked up, it made a good load for two horses, although it was bulky in part, ornaments and such, as Talley commented.

"We'll go then," I said. "Did you get it all?"

Degory shrugged. "There's some odds and ends down there, a few coins . . . maybe a ring or so. We didn't want to scrabble in the dark for them."

"I know, Deg. You were thinking of Van Runkle."

"Well, the man's looked for a long time. Let him have what he finds, Lucinda won't miss it."

We rode away in the breaking dawn, our horses' hooves and the creak of saddles our only sound.

When from the rise of the pass I glanced back, turning in my saddle to look, it was all merged into one, gray and green and lovely, with a mist on the lowlands.

Somewhere over the horizon were the Mandan villages, and although I had no furs and the treasure we carried was not mine, I rode with hard memories grown softer with time, a new lust for life within me, and the Ferguson rifle over my saddle.

And, of course, there was Lucinda.